Fear in the Face of a Dying Dream

Masterpiece: Volume 1

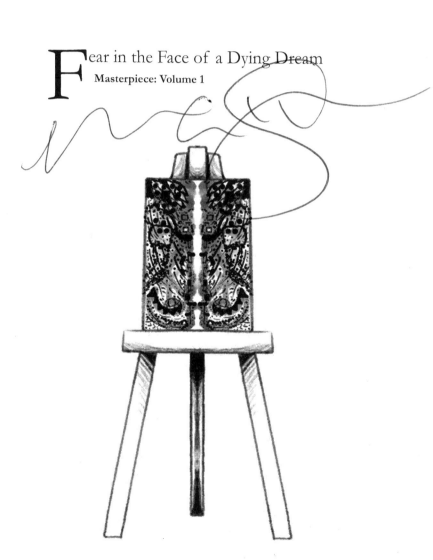

Authored by Matthew Sawyer

Illistration by Israel

Cover Art collaboration by Laura and Israel

Acknowledgments:

I always thought my purpose was to be a musician. I never in a million years thought I would ever write a book. Mainly because I never read a book really. Growing up I just couldn't concentrate on reading long enough to finish a book. I had the idea pop into my head when I lost my voice in a rock band and needed to explore other avenues of my artistry.

First of all, I want to give an eternal thanks to my wife Paula Bernette. Before we were married six years before I wrote this book, I was headed down a road of addictive, destructive drug usage. My wife was exactly what I needed to bring the best out of me, including giving me two beautiful children, Kavi Rayne, and Matthew Kai. We hope to have more children in the future which I also want to thank in advance for being exactly who they will become. I want to thank my entire family especially my brothers and sisters for playing a great role in my life. I thank my entire family for always being there for me and supporting me in my continuing journey in life. Despite our differences, they were always there for me. I want to thank my dad, Jim, for instilling valuable standards and expectations in life and always being there for guidance despite our differences. I want to thank my mother Wendy for always being selfless and loving. Without her love, I would not be who I am today. Next, I want to thank my friend Justin for always being supportive and my best friend of 15 years and counting!

I want to give a special thanks to Isaac Beckett for delivering a beautiful artistic edit on this book. I also thank Isaac for encouraging me to expand the book to its fullest potential. Isaac has always been my biggest fan as a musician and as a writer. He always made me feel like I have a lot of talent. Isaac, being such an intelligent person, had a huge effect on my confidence as a writer and artist.

Next, I want to give a beautiful thank you to Laura Short with Venture Studio, LLC in Oklahoma City. Thank you for being such a talented designer with the book cover, back, and binding. She also helped me write the description on the back of the book. Laura has always been there to help me in my artistic endeavors. She truly is gifted in her craft and a valued friend. I also want to thank her husband Elliott Short for always being a brilliant mind to come to for advice, from software development to everyday practical outlooks. I specifically want to thank him for helping me create an online marketplace to sell digital copies of the book and future developments.

I want to give a special thanks to my cousins Rodrick and Rebekah for always believing in me and being there for me. Rodrick has been a special friend that I have called with many issues and he has always been a helping hand despite his own battles in life.

I need to give a special thanks to my best friend and brother Israel Doll who actually sparked a portion on the storyline by letting me into intimate pain and struggles in his childhood. Israel has been a trusted friend that has always been there for support and guidance. I also want to thank Israel for doing the basic edit on this book and overall support.

Also, the characters in the book were inspired by true events in people in my life. Corrina Hardeman who I got mad love for. She's been a great friend and I thank her for letting me into her personal medical issues that inspired a story that will help many. There was a guy named Seth who I don't know personally, but let me into trauma in his childhood I was able to help him with.

Lastly, I want to thank God for leading me on my journey and gifting me with the talent of writing and artistry. I've always told my friends while I was in the process of writing this book "I can take the credit for writing the book, but I can't take credit for the story." I believe God has led me through my life with a complex understanding and view on life and concept of God and religion. I give credit to God and the missing link that connects me to him personally. Part of the artistry of this book is finding out what the missing link is in your life specifically, whatever that may be. My personal beliefs aside, whatever the deep truths of life are, I believe this book can be a tool in finding the truth and the missing link. Thank you to all who will read this book and I want you to know what an honor it is to be able to write a book and share it with all who pick it up.

Table of Contents:

The Preface:

As I stare into my canvas, I see how each brush stroke makes such a difference. Every time I change my mind on the direction, I realize that every stroke has a specific purpose, a place in the overall painting. For the greater good, I should say. What if I randomly splatter a pointless stroke of disaster? Another way I could look at this question is, could this be nothing more than a stroke of luck? Oh, that's good. Wait, that couldn't work, unless... I make it work, of course. Interesting concept, I like this concept rather well actually.

See, we all have these expectations in life, these labeled boxes that we put our personal experiences in. What a beautiful picture of how we all play a personal role, a personal part in this story we call life. The proof is that we do all have different expectations, don't we? Great! We agree on this matter then. This reminds me of my whole point. Humanity, please bear with me, as I know we're all tired of the cliche philosophical "RA-RA" that were unbelievably used to in life. However, humanity is all we as a race seem to understand on a surface level. Perhaps, your perception of humanity is only a figment of your imagination. I feel the word "imagination" comes across too colorful in this context. I think "desire" may better express what I mean. A "desire" to better understand ourselves as humans is what we all simultaneously are trying to accomplish.

This brings me to my secondary point. See, I think... no, I "desire" that there is more to the human race than what meets the naked eye. I encourage you to read this "Preface" three times to grasp the three levels of understanding this "Preface" contains. You read it once now, once before chapter seven, and for the third time at the end of the book. Ultimately, it's up to you if you re-read or not. My tri-angular point in the opening of this book, or maybe it's more of an offer to you as the individual reader, is to follow me into my dream, my masterpiece painting of a canvas. Literally, with your hearts permission, I will take you on a journey to the center of the canvas. This canvas is you. This canvas is me. Your experiences are the strokes of the brush that provide the colors of your life. Be warned! Don't get lost or lose your way as this is an artistic journey. Try and keep up in the first two chapters as they do move at a very fast pace to not only what the tri-eye can see, but what is beyond deep, deep into the subconscious of what you "perceive" as the human race. Still, as humanity remains a singular consciousness, separated by personal but very unique energetic entities, this is exactly as strange as you "perceive" it to be. Still, I ask to follow me into the colorful life of a boy named Kevin.

The Shotgun Setting:
Chapter 0

Each stroke he makes is thorough, precise, and confident. He has a natural ability to make treasure out of trash. As what goes up must come down, so does each stroke of his knife serve a specific purpose. See, Kevin started carving wood when he was seven years old. As his bedroom dresser fills up with finished carvings of bears, eagles, trees and many other beautiful sculptures, his dad Abraham, had no choice but to give Kevin his Grandpa's "William Henry Spearpoint Trek" heirloom pocket knife. This knife was a special knife for a special boy on his 10th birthday.

Four years have passed by since that gift was given. Nowadays, Kevin is passed that first major growth spurt. He started shaving his wispy sideburns and continues to shave his peach fuzz beard off, for normal teenage egotistical reasons of course. He's a handsome young man. He's very tall but skinny as his arms and legs are very long and look like spaghetti. He's proud his voice has deepened, however, it still cracks like a slide whistle from time to time. Despite all these stages of His adolescence, nothing stops him from carving wood like a grown man. Slowly his dresser collection of animal carvings had turned into a huge wooden chest collection, Kevin began to desire more from his own artistry. Slam! Kevin heard the front door crash in an unusual fashion.

"Something is off," Kevin thought to himself.

Just as he was striking his blade against blunt wooden objects, he quickly and skillfully tiptoed across the upstairs hallway and sat at the top of the staircase to curiously watch and listen. As soon as Kevin peeked his head through the spindles on the top step he noticed his dad drop the mail on the kitchen counter as he normally did when he got home from work. He didn't seem angry. His mom Jazmine, was washing dishes next to his dad when Kevin heard his dad ask a very typical question,

"So… how did your day go?"

Kevin usually is not this nosy, he has much better things to do with his time, like listening to punk rock music or flexing his muscles in the mirrors. After all, he is fourteen now and well… he's just in the prime of his life.

Lately, his mom and dad have been acting strange. He's so used to going to the mall every Saturday afternoon or having family movie night every Friday. Kevin knows his family isn't perfect but his family is "unbreakable," just like Bruce Willis from M. Night's greatest film. Most of Kevin's friends are at the stage where they hate their parents and just complain about how they want to be away from their family and just kick it. Kevin always kept his opinion about his family to himself because that would keep him from fitting in. It just seems like everyone's been a little distant lately. Now that Kevin is thinking about everything, he realizes Abraham has been working a new job in the big city. See, they just moved from Oklahoma

City to Denver Colorado.

"It must be a 'rough transition' kind of thing," Kevin thought to himself.

Then his mom responded to his dad, "I brought the papers from the courthouse, they are on your desk to sign."

Kevin thought to himself, "Courthouse?" He continued this train of thought, "What business does she have in the courthouse?"

Still, every question he had about his parents remained unresolved. Exhausted, from so much missing information Kevin decided to go back to his room to make some more strokes on his new project.

Okay, pause!

Now, remember, we are in my painting of a canvas, and as I asked you to follow me before. I'm asking you to follow me down into the downstairs kitchen so you can hear the rest of the dialogue between Abraham and Jazmine. Use your "imagination" or "desire." Whichever word you relate to most and walk discreetly, as we saw Kevin walk discreetly.

Stop! That's far enough, for now, just listen...

Abraham asks Jazmine in a monotone type of voice. "So, how are we going to do this?"

"Do what?" Jazmine asked.

Abraham mumbled under his breath "Tell our children about the divorce?"

I did forget to mention that Kevin has two sisters, named Carrie and Seymer, that are five and seven. Jazmine began to share what she believed to be the conclusion of thoughtful energy and wisdom.

She started by sharing with her soon to be ex-husband Abraham, "Well you're the man and Kevin is our eldest son," Jazmine explained, "I think you should tell him first. Then, after Kevin has come to accept our divorce, hopefully, he'll be ready to help Carrie and Seymer understand. We will all three together explain to the girls about co-parenting and how this all works. We will explain How you will live in another house and our children will live with us equally."

Abraham takes a deep breath and replies, "Should we try and give counseling more time before we..."

"Abraham, stop!" Jazmine yelled.

"Mom," Kevin poked his head out of his upstairs bedroom and asked... "Is everything okay? Why are you yelling?"

Jazmine replies, "Son, everything's fine. Me and your dad are just discussing bills."

This actually made sense in Kevin's mind, when he remembered the stack of mail his dad put on the counter after he slammed the door. So he took her word for it and returned to his work.

When Jazmine heard Kevin's door close she continues in a stern but quiet voice, "Abraham, I will always cherish the memories we share, and I'm thankful for our kids but we both know this is over."

Abraham lowers his head in pain. Jazmine continued to make her case. "We will co-parent. You will continue to be a great father and we will both move on and put the past behind us."

Abraham replied "I GET IT, I get it, let me talk to him. You're right... it is over and it would be nice to have him help the girls understand since your mind is obviously made up."

Jazmine persisted, "My mind has been made up for a long time now and this talk is long overdue, so please, let's get this over with so we can get a new routine going with the family."

Okay, pause!

Now, as your reading this, I'll use the word "imagine" or the word "desire..." Let us "Imagine" Abraham heading upstairs… Okay? Just as he passes us standing in the hallway between the kitchen and the staircase, he feels something strange. Like something is watching. You know, that feeling we all get from time to time, like something is watching? Yeah, I knew you would recognize that feeling to some degree. Well, now you know what it's like to be on the other side of things. You know what it's like to be the one who's watching. Anyhow, he continues upstairs and we should follow. So be sure to keep up, come, come...

Creeeeeeekkkkkk

Those old doors are not as discrete as I am, almost no one realizes when I'm with them. I say to you as my follower and the reader, Let us float right through the gap between Abraham and the door, to get a better picture of what happens next.

"Hey, kid," Abraham began, "I see you're using Papa's knife still. How's it holding up after all the years?"

"I keep it sharp," Kevin explained, "and it really helps with the details of everything. I could have never carved a rabbit with my old knife, not to mention this whole family of rabbits."

"I see," Abraham murmured under his breath, he couldn't help but think of the news he was about to deliver to his boy.

"Dad," Kevin said in a throbbing voice.

"Yes, Kev?" Abraham noticed Kevin had a tear run down his right cheek, which just so happens to be the cheek Kevin has a noticeably adorable dimple.

"Dad, remember when I mowed our yard last summer after the grass hadn't been cut for so long the grass was almost knee high?"

"Yes," Abraham responded.

"Well, I've been having dreams of that rabbit's nest I accidentally hit with our mower. It's been three nights in a row now. The only way I feel I can have some closure is to make a wooden statue of the babies I killed. Is that stupid?"

Abraham smiled in pride over his son and sternly said "No... Kev, you are so strong for allowing yourself to be vulnerable. That's part of being a man, you're growing up, I'm proud of you and don't let that accident get in your head. It wasn't your fault. Things like that happen sometimes." Abraham continued, "Son, there's something we need to talk about."

Kevin quickly got a concerned look on his face and asked, "What is it? Am I in trouble?"

Abraham gave a strange chuckle and said "No, son. It's nothing to do with you. It's just..."

As Abraham hesitated, Kevin got irritated and interrupted, "Just what, dad!?"

Abraham immediately buckled under pressure and exclaimed, "Just don't let the grass get that high again and you'll be alright."

They both had a good laugh and Abraham scuffed up his son's hair and walked away.

Pause!

I need to "pause" once again because pausing is the best way to help you keep up with the bigger picture. The overall painting of this canvas that is you, Kevin and I. You, as the viewer should be pretty curious about my primary point in the preface, which is "expectations." I led you to "believe" or "expect" Abraham was going to tell his son about the divorce in this brush stroke of Kevin's experience, right? Or was it your perception of Kevin's experience that blurred the lines? You're doing well keeping up on this journey. Stay close to my voice and you won't get lost as we venture down the rabbit hole.

After all, you have been warned, "Don't get lost."

So, let's continue inside my masterpiece painting of a canvas, shall we?

The Last Supper:

Chapter 1

Jazmine always had the ability to make a good homecooked meal. This has always brought the family together. She moves faster than she should be able to move with her short legs. She brings the last plate of food to the kitchen table as Abraham was outside chopping wood. She secretly fixes her curly dark hair in the mirror and then walks briskly to the kitchen window and struggles to slide that old wooden window up.

Crack!

Despite her petite body mass, She's a firecracker! She broke the window free as she did several times before to let her husband know it's time to eat.

Jazmine yells, "Abraham, come to the table, dinner is ready!"

Abraham responds, "Get the kids first, I'm almost finished with this tree."

Abraham is a hard worker. He makes Paul Bunyan look like a bedtime story, with how he swings that ax with such precision.

You can see where Kevin gets his skill from just by watching his father cut wood.

Jazmine yells "Girls! Kevin! Come to the table."

Almost immediately you hear Carrie and Seymer's little feet shuffle down the stairs giggling. The girls are always so happy. It's like kids that never run out of candy, even though that's not the case. This family isn't big on sugar, to say the least. The girls are just "high on life" you could say. With the eye-sparkle only a happy child can have. Carrie is older with the same curly hair as her mom. She gets so many compliments on her hereditary dimples and freckles. It's so frustrating how many times the girls hear that they are twins from strangers.

"Oh, my goodness! What cute twins!" people say.It's a constant dialogue to explain how their two years apart.

"Kevin! Come downstairs, please! This is the last time I'll ask before I drag you down myself!"

Jazmine has such a funny sense of humor despite all the changes the family is about to go through. It's that kind of morbid sense of humor. Kevin understands she's kidding but very serious at the same time. So, Kevin continues the shuffling stair steps as Carrie and Seymer are playing with their dolls at the table. Abraham steps in and shuts the door. Time stops for Abraham as His beautiful family is all at the table staring at him.

"Hi, Daddy," Carrie says.

"Daddy!" Seymer follows her sisters lead.

Abraham responds, "Hi, babies."

Carrie insists, "We're not babies anymore, Daddy," even though she secretly likes it when her Daddy calls her baby.

Kevin notices his dad's face looks off, but it's so hard to tell with half of his face covered with that thick burly type of a beard. Kevin always looked up to his dad. He's so strong. He has always been there in Kevin's life. He has always appreciated his dad. Kevin's dad was clear in letting him know how much he loved him. After all, his father showed Kevin how to love, by loving his family right in front of him all these years he's been alive.

Abraham asks, "Can you pass the lamb please Carrie?"

Carrie says, "Daddy…"

Abraham responds, "Yes, Carrie?"

Next Carrie speaks in a facetious manner, "You didn't Pray."

Abraham smiles and begins the ritualistic prayer his Dad's Dad said before him.

"Now can you pass the lamb please, Carrie."

"Yes, Daddy," Carrie says giggling as she reaches for the plate full of meat.

After all the food makes it around the table. Kevin, still thinking about how something is off with his dad, begins fidgeting with his food.

"Kevin, what's wrong? Eat your food please," Jazmine said.

Kevin avoids all confrontation at this point and begins to eat. Things were quiet at the table for a while until the girls broke the silence as little girls do so well. Somehow, Seymer got a hold of Carrie's baby doll. Angrily, Carrie begins a tug of war battle with her sister. When Seymer suddenly fell out of the chair, Abraham snaps!

SLAM!

His big fist shook the table.

Abraham's voice doesn't usually get loud, but he chose to let it out saying, "Dammit, girls! Sit down and eat."

Jazmine yells back "Abraham!"

Abraham decides to stand his ground. It felt good to Abraham. Acting out in such a manner makes him feel some level of control in the house again. Even though everything in his world is crumbling around him.

Abraham makes his case by stating, "We can have peace at the table... or I will remove myself."

Jazmine, thinking about how this will be the last meal as a family and is very upset.

Jazmine gently touches his hand and sternly says, "Abraham, I don't know what has gotten into you, but I think it's best you remove yourself."

Abraham storms out to the backyard after he grabbed the bottle of wine out of the upper cabinet and slammed the door.

Kevin notices this is the third slam he's heard today. Frustrated at the chaos, Kevin asks his mom if he can be excused.

Jazmine responds, "Yes, son."

Kevin begins to get up and Jazmine continues, "Kevin!"

Kevin replies, "Yes, Mom?"

"Take your food upstairs and eat please."

Kevin looks down at his plate and responds, "Yes, ma'am." Even though he had no intention of touching the food as his stomach was turning inside, he knew something was up.

Pause!

Now, remember in this painting we can do whatever we want. For now, we're going to follow Kevin upstairs, but before we do, I want to point out the last thing Kevin hears as he's going upstairs.

Jazmine begins to say to Carrie and Seymer, "How about ice cream?"

The girls go from sad, because of their dad's behavior, to screaming in joy, "Ice cream! Ice cream!"

That's when Kevin really got concerned, his mom keeps the family on an extremely low sugar diet excluding carbs. She almost never takes anyone in the family out for ice cream.

Un-pause!

Now don't trip over these old wooden steps, and let's make sure to squeeze in before he shuts the door. This next part of my painting is a difficult stroke of the brush to accept. However, it serves a specific purpose in the overall painting. It was hard for me to allow this. Like a battle within myself, I claim to be the artist of the whole story, not just the happy parts but also how the hard parts in life that tend to create the best types of endings. Without further ado, let me introduce you to a very close partner of my existence. A new character, if you will. Let's just call this character "The Mime." The Mime is such a beautiful piece of work. Always working everywhere, in everyone's life simultaneously. Strange right? So powerful this soft spirited entity is. Dressed in a form-fitting white gown with hieroglyphics scattered through her dress, radiating bright turquoise energetic patterns, the Mime is already doing its work, interpreting this scene through expressive dancing. The Mime is so feminine, in my humble opinion. So passionate in its work. Always there in every human experience even when I don't mention its presence. Even when I don't mention my own presence.

As Kevin begins finishing up this carving of this family of rabbits. The Mime begins taking position in Kevin's closest corner and sits down starting to cry. Such a compassionate spirit the mime is, dancing, radiating healing for the good of everyone who stands, but I've only given you partial information as another entity named Tusk awaits in the corner as Kevin's dad covers this entity up by opening the door.

Abraham slurs, "Kevin."

Kevin noticed his dad stumbled in, "You're drunk, Dad."

Abraham decided to get straight to the point in a very cold manner. "Son, me and your mom are getting a divorce. You're the eldest son so, I thought you should know first. Tomorrow we'll be telling the girls and could use your help explaining this to them."

Abraham then turns around and softly shuts the door behind himself.

Kevin yells, "You're drunk, Dad!"

Then he throws the family of rabbits at the door with all his energy. Kevin begins pacing back and forth with racing thoughts. Anxiety is the word that comes to mind; however, Kevin is too young to recognize this.

"How could this be? Not me." Kevin thought to himself.

This was such a dark-edged shock. Why wouldn't it be a shock to Kevin, as he always felt his family was strong and solid? Kevin continues to catch up with his thoughts.

"How can I let my sisters find out about this? My sweet baby sisters' lives are about to be ruined. They will crumble."

Kevin felt extremely responsible for holding this information hostage. This wave of emotions begins drowning Kevin and then it quickly turns into a wave of fear. At this point, he grips his dark coarse hair in between his fingers and pulls his eyelids shut. He thought his hair was about to rip out of his head as he realized the pain seemed to distract him from the constant mental confusion he was experiencing for the first time in his life. This pain seemed to have a numbing effect on these mental emotions. Like a drug, he understood the enjoyment of pain just like he understood the enjoyment of carving wood. This was far too much for Kevin.

The Mime begins to stand up slowly with her head in a downward motion.

Pause!

Now, remember the downward motion of the Mime's head after I say the word "play." What I did not mention is that when Abraham shut the door, this other entity, Tusk, dressed like a clean-cut businessman emerged. He presses his hands together and rubs them back and forth and starts walking towards Kevin. Remember the position of the Mimes head? Okay...

Play!

The Mime begins to lift its head up facing and staring straight at Tusk. As tears run down the face of the Mime it begins to burst out in powerful but passionate dancing until Tusk sits next to Kevin. Then the Mime knows its comfort is needed. Kevin is sitting on the floor with his back on the side of his bed, and the Mime chooses to take the position of sitting on the mattress of the bed with one leg on each side of Kevin's body. The Mime is Caressing his face and still is crying. Kevin's fear quickly turns into a deep, dark depression. An ocean-like wave of depression hit Kevin like a surfer hits the rocks after a wipeout. He doesn't recognize this depression like he recognizes his racing thoughts of how he could not solve this problem.

"Nothing..." Kevin thought to himself, "There's simply nothing."

His world was crushed. Everything he believed in was about to be taken from him. Little does Kevin know about the presence of Tusk, the Mime and I. Kevin also doesn't realize this entity, Tusk, is sitting on the floor to his right side. Kevin had an end table next to his bed to his left side where he kept all his carving tools. Tusk slithers his arm around Kevin and chills begin to go down his spine so fast Kevin begins to shake and tremble. Tusk quickly leans over and whisper powerful energetic thoughts through Kevin's body and senses. Overstimulated by this energy suddenly passing through him, he slams his fist against his forehead. At that moment Kevin turns and looks at his heirloom knife and reaches for it. Shaking his head, and tears pouring down his face, he rips his sleeve up to his elbows. Without hesitation, just as precisely as he strikes blunt wooden pieces, he strikes precisely in a horizontal motion on his beautifully colored forearm. This cut was not a cry for attention. This cut was not planned... it just happened.

He dropped the knife and realized it was over. The blood ran slower than he expected for how deep the cut was. He enjoyed the release he felt, taking all these emotions out on something that felt so dead. This blood made him realize how alive he really was when it went from slow bleeding to gushing all over his body. As his breathing slowed, the blood had drenched his pants already. The Mime was still patiently caressing Kevin's face and crying.

Tusk briskly stands up in front of Kevin with a questionable grin on his face. Tusk can feel Kevin's pulse slowing down and begins to feel excited to see his prey fading out. Tusk saw Kevin's eyes rolling to the back of his head, and at this moment Tusk leans over Kevin's face and looks him directly in the eyes. For a split-second, Kevin could see tusk glaring at him before he loses consciousness. Remember that Kevin did see Tusk's face before he passed out.

Darkness overtook this happy, normal teenage boy just twenty minutes ago. How could such a horrific scenario play out in such a short amount of time with such a drastic outcome? Kevin was too young. He had never experienced any form of mental illness. Strong anxiety, fear, and depression hit him in a matter of minutes. Some powerful entity has taken advantage of the normal realities unfolding around Kevin. The realities that are around all of us. Kevin had no idea the battle he was facing. It was too late for him to have second thoughts. His life was soon to be over.

Pause!

I know that explaining this so plainly sounds cold. Remember this is my painting, my canvas. I'm in control and I know the entirety of the story. I can see Kevin's body in many layers. I don't just see his skin. I can see his cartilage and ligaments; I can see his brain activity. I can see his overactive neurons are firing more than they ever have before. At the front middle part of his brain, I can see what is called the pineal gland. This gland holds all his DMT. This DMT I speak of is responsible for all our deep layers of our dreams. Your outer layer of sleep is called your R.E.M. sleep. This R.E.M. sleep is only the hallucinatory, "aftereffects" of DMT. DMT plays a major role not only in your deepest part of sleep which you cannot remember but also DMT is responsible for near our death experiences. I should mention DMT is in just about all living organisms; plants, trees, animals, etc. Anything that's alive and growing possesses this amazing connection called DMT. Let's just say It's very possible this is the portal to the next life and much more than what we humans understand.

As I looked into his pineal gland, I can see a flood of DMT

travel through neural pathways, over stimulating his brain's potential. Again, as I asked you to follow me before. I ask you to Follow me again, not only beyond your perception of the human race but into the deep, deep subconscious.

This is as strange as you perceive it to be but don't let that scare you off.

Come, come, follow me.

Be warned!

Don't get lost in this journey to the center of my masterpiece painting of a canvas. This canvas is you, and the brush strokes of paint, are your experiences and expectations of what you and me both call life. As much as I enjoy being the artist of this masterpiece painting, there comes a time when the artist needs to take a step back and wait. Look and see for yourself, see how all the paint on this canvas is so fresh? What happens when the paint dries as I walk away and tend to my other projects? I will come back when the time is right and finish what I started one way or another. I will finish my painting myself or through someone else. For now, I will remain in this next chapter and all the chapters to come even when I'm not seen or spoken of. However, everything you read is now from Kevin's perspective. I have enjoyed the introduction and letting you into my mind and the way I think but I deeply care for Kevin as I deeply care for you. The main point is, this is Kevin's DMT experience. So here it goes, let's "imagine," or "desire" the switch to begin...

The Hallway:

Chapter 2

Ting ting...cling cling. I bounce around this metal dinner triangle with a long metal cylinder to get the birds to chirp again. Ahh, there we go it's so nice to hear the birds start to sing. What a beautiful sound. So pleasantly birds fly through the sky with such elegance. "As light as a feather," is a term my dad uses a lot around me. I see why I can't fly with how heavy I feel, stepping on the red squares only, avoiding all these annoying cracks. Call me O.C.D. but I enjoy this rather well. It's the kind of tile floors you see in the grocery store white and red checkered squares. Forward I move and I refuse to step on a crack. It would just make me cringe. One square after another I move forward.

"Kevin come here."

Hmmm... I've never heard this voice before as I still focus on not hitting any cracks, only stepping on the red tiles.

"Kevin, don't you remember me?"

"Dang it!" I yelled.

There it goes. I officially lost my focus. The crack has been stepped on.

"I swear I'm not going to be happy with whoever distracted me. I should be focusing my attention on the tiles right now, not lifting my head to see..."

Hmmm... How strange, I do not recognize his voice, but his face is oddly familiar. Almost as if I was just looking at him not too long ago. He had a black fedora on and a gray curly mustache. His suit was sharp and form-fitting. Black with white pinstripes all the way down to his shiny shoes, so shiny I could see my reflection. What a nice old man he appears to be. Not too old, and he clearly is some kind of businessman with that fancy suit. He had a desk with some papers sitting on it. I couldn't see what was on the papers. He wasn't at his desk actually. He was relaxing on a red leather chair with a very tall chair back. It was like he was watching me play my "don't step on the crack game" the whole time. With one leg crossed over the other leg, he was tapping his foot on a dark fur rug with a fireplace blazing behind him.

He had a huge flat screen TV on the wall with a show on it that caught my attention more than his familiar look. This show had a man that appeared to be in his twenties carving a blunt piece of wood into a family of bunnies. What a coincidence, I too have many carvings and my latest carving was, in fact, a family of bunnies. I must go talk to this man. This is clearly a sign and meant to be. Every step I made closer to this man, he began to repeat himself saying,

"Yes, come, child... come, child, I have a great deal for you. A deal you can't refuse."

He must be interested in my skills carving wood clearly, considering the show he was playing on his TV. With each step I get closer I notice his fool tap faster and faster. When I was about seven feet away his foot was tapping so fast I thought he was having a seizure.

"My name is Tusk. What is your name?" His foot stopped abruptly.

Something was drawing me to him. I felt like he could help me be who I was meant to be. I was still the same distance away and just as I was about to tell him my name, I felt a briskly strong but gentle arm around my shoulder. Pressing down hard enough on my right side it made me spin around like a ballerina from the Nutcracker.

"Hello, Kevin," this man said in a comforting voice.

It's like he already knew me, I mean come on! The irony of Tusk asking me my name made me realize Tusk was obviously less informed than this mystery man was. It was strange, right as I was about to tell Tusk my name, this random man called me. Not only did he call me but he called me by name. That was enough to capture my attention and explore what he had to say to me.

His face did not match his voice like I expected. He had a white V-neck t-shirt on with colorful gypsy pants with all kinds of geometrical patterns on it. Rope sandals covered his feet, I couldn't help but notice his long piano toes. That face though, he had huge turquoise eyes, there were no whites to his eyes, just pure turquoise with a pearl-like glaze over them. I was lost in these beautiful deep eyes. He had long pure white hair down to his knees all braided into one huge clump. His sideburns poured out from the side of his face like chicken noodle soup. He had a strong chin with a dimple right in the center and with the straightest teeth you've ever seen. I was in awe. Then, he just glared into my eyes. He just stared at me. His enormous turquoise eyes glared at me. He was not glaring in a scary way. It was like he was looking into my soul, and I was looking into his.

"What's your name?" I asked.

He replied "I will give you a formal introduction, however, for now, just stare into my eyes. I have something I want to tell you," He continued, "Kevin, not all friendly faces are friendly faces."

I was a bit confused if he was referring to himself or the nice businessman at the end of the hallway. He made no attempt to defend himself one way or the other.

"Walk with me," he insisted, "Walk with me not just for the moment, but also for what's beyond the moment."

He kept his arm around me and led me forward. It drove me crazy stepping all over the cracks of the tiles, but he led me with such authority I decided to look up to his face and admire his interesting appearance instead of playing my O.C.D. "crack stepping game." This was a bit difficult with how short he was, so I ended up looking eye level with him. See, I'm tall for my age, sitting at 5'9, but he was a full-grown man so like I said, I was at eye level. This was nice for a change.I was used to looking up to my dad, who probably stood at 6'5. It always made me feel like I had a long way to go before I could be eye level with him.

We were walking the opposite direction of the businessman, in this extremely long and colorful hallway. Birds were singing and the walls were covered in what appeared to be shiny glitter and precious stones. It was so beautiful I couldn't decide to give my attention to him or this beautifully designed hallway. It wasn't a normal rectangular shaped hallway like I was used to. It was multidimensional, like the ceilings were multidimensional as if it were the blueprints of a cylinder for some contractor that worked for a very artistic designer.

Then he asked me, "Kevin, let me say, do you happen to be a painter of a masterpiece canvas?"

I thought to myself what a strange question, "Umm, no, not really," I responded.

"May I ask how you have come to that conclusion, Kevin?"

"Well, because I've never painted before. I assumed I wouldn't be good at it, I guess. What I consider myself to be good at is carving wood into all kinds of animals, you know?"

"I see, so is your knife not the same as a brush and the wood the same as a canvas?"

I responded, "I mean, I guess, if that is your perception, but you asked me if I was a painter and the answer is no. I'm sorry if that disappoints you."

"Kevin, you don't have the power to disappoint me because

I can see you. This is why I look into your eyes and told you to look into my eyes because 'the eyes are the window to the soul.'"

I thought to myself, "There's some more irony, as I just had come to this conclusion on my own."

The strange man continued to share, "However, you mention 'perception', such an interesting choice of words. I believe perception is what makes everything you see as reality become your actual reality... you see, perceptions, this is exactly what makes reality real." He continued, "What if I told you 'perception' is the tool you use to create, and the canvas you use to create really doesn't hold any significance, only that you use this tool to create?"

This sounds familiar, like I've heard this a few times, but I couldn't quite put my finger on it.

So, I responded, "I guess that makes sense from your perspective, but what does it mean?"

He replied, "What does it mean? Now that's a very good question! Unfortunately, that's a question I cannot answer for you. You have to find the inner strength to face all the battles in front of you to find the answer to that question."

I asked curiously, "What kind of battles are you talking about?"

He responded, "Battles you have to face, Kevin... to become the man you want to be, the man you're meant to be."

I thought to myself, "The man I'm meant to be?"

So, I asked, "How do you know the man I'm meant to be?"

"Kevin, I know this because I'm an artist as well, I have a masterpiece painting of my own that I'm working on and I have had hard battles I had to face along the way. The free will of all my art is the hardest part to accept, but also, it's the most rewarding. A lot of the adversities on the canvas were heart-wrenching for me to accept. The pain of people I deeply loved, people I choose to create in my paintings, this broke my heart. This hurt me, but I can see the bigger picture and I knew I had to face these battles. So I ask you, are you willing to face your battles?"

Normally, I would not entertain these conversations, but something about what he was saying made sense to me. So I responded, "I suppose I'm willing to face these battles, but what do I need to do?"

He laughed and gently said, "What do you need to do? Trust in me, and every word I say. That is all I ask of you."

At this point we made it to the end of the hallway, to the door I entered, right at the beginning when I rang the dinner bell to make the birds sing again. When I looked around, I noticed three doors. Every door had a padlock, but the padlocks were all unlocked. My mind began racing, thinking, "I thought was strange, I had some red flags going off up in my brain, but still I remained in his mind another day. It's probably me, though. I'm just going insane. It's probably me…"

"STOP THINKING KEVIN!" I thought to myself as I

started to calm myself down.

"Whew," I almost lost it. I took a deep breath and continued to observe. Every door had an old-fashioned torch hanging on the right side of every door. The torch was lit with a flame that drew me in. I began to reach for the flame to touch it as I felt one with this fire for some reason. As I stretched my hand out the man quickly interrupted the trance I was in and said "Stop! Kevin this door is for you, this flame is for another time. It seemed like everything was set up here for a purpose.

I was confused about what was going on, then the strange man said to me, "Kevin, I want you to go through The Fear Room first. You subconsciously avoid the concept of fear most, as do most people in the world. Fear is a very complex issue as it takes many forms and it can hit you from many angles. Sometimes you don't even know you're afraid. I know right now you're afraid, but I want you to know everything will be okay. I'm in control you can trust me."

Something inside was wanting to believe him, but I was still afraid. I couldn't seem to let go of my fear.

He said, "Kevin, I have a gift for you."

Then he pulled out a cylinder that was made out of the most beautiful diamonds I had ever seen. I was curious as to where these diamonds came from as they were no ordinary diamonds. Words cannot describe its beauty; they were simply indescribable.

He continued, "This is your tool to see the truth of The Fear

Room. Also, this is the only way you can see me, as I am only allowed to be in truthful places. So, if you want to talk with me, all have to do is look through this cylinder scope. We can talk anytime you're afraid or anytime you're not. You get to decide when to use this tool. In this room, you will be an observer and an investigator of how fear works. Gaining this knowledge of fear will help you through the doors to come. There will a door master

behind every door and this one will be aware of your presence, but she will not interfere with your free will, as I will be with you. She is powerless, so observe and go wherever you want knowing she can't hurt you. Also, know I'm walking beside you the entire time."

"What should I call you?"

He responded in a solid, strong voice and said, "I have many names, but for you and for this painting I decide to formally, give my name as 'The Narrator'."

I thought about what he was saying and felt relieved he was going through the door with me. I stared at The Door of Fear and felt afraid, of course. I looked at the door and it was beautiful. It was made out of solid gold and had carvings kind of like hieroglyphics, except it was just artistry. Indescribable artistry. Nothing about this door looked scary. So, with much confidence, I looked at my new friend and we smiled at each other and stepped through.

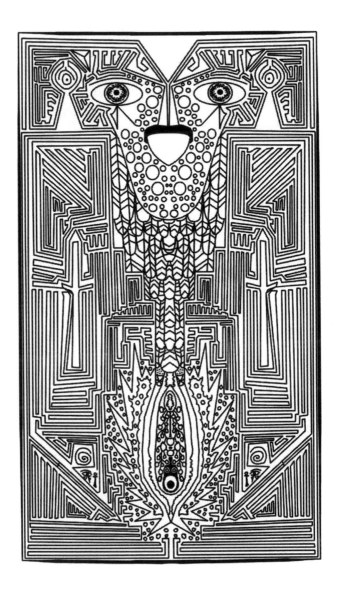

The Illusion:

Chapter 3

My first thought in stepping through The Door of Fear was to be afraid. Immediately, as I began to walk forward my vision became clear. I was in a very beautiful room and my attention went straight to this thrown. On this throne sat a young beautiful princess or queen and she was staring right at me. It was almost like we were in some kind of fancy ballroom at a queen's palace or something. Everyone was dancing and eating fancy food. Everyone seemed to be enjoying themselves rather well. I was a bit confused as to why this was called "The Fear Room."

The beautiful woman made a movement towards me with such beauty and elegance. Her face lit up with seductive beauty that drew me in. My feelings for her grew with each step she got closer. When she got within arm's reach she smiled and spun around me putting her hand on my neck. She smelled of perfume and was covered in shiny glitter all over her body. Her black dress made it difficult to look at her legs or the beauty of her face. As she looked into my eyes she began to speak.

"Welcome to my palace boy, my name is Shanti." She said, in

a sweet voice. "Please sit next to me on my altar."

As I sat and stared at her she continued "Look around, I want you to see...to see the happiness of my company. They are such a peculiar company, aren't they? All they care about is the beauty they can see with their eyes and feel with their hands. I'm so happy I have the ability to satisfy their every desire. Am I not royal? Am I not wonderful?"

I hesitated and gave a little chuckle. She cut me off before I had the chance to answer and she said, "Kiss me, boy. Kiss me and become a part of my company."

I got very nervous and start fidgeting with my pockets and felt the cylinder scope the narrator gave me and immediately jumped out of excitement. I can't believe I forgot he was with me! I was mesmerized by the beauty, but because I knew there was an evil Door Master, suddenly I felt very uncomfortable. I took my scope out to find the narrator as the princess walked towards her throne and sat down. I looked at the scope for a few more moments and then put my eyes to the end of the scope.

SNAP!

Just like that, golden tapestry turned to concrete walls and greasy floors. LIKE A DUNGEON! I felt the pressure of reality hitting me. The people were no longer scattered around the room but all in rows chained to one another. They seemed to be in some kind of a trance. They stood in one place and rocked back and forth with their eyes glazed over like a snake about to shed its skin. They were paralyzed.

"Fear is not always as it appears to be." I recognized this voice immediately to be my lovely new friend, The Narrator.

I was terrified. All the people huddled together just gave me the creeps, so I said, "Narrator, what happened? Why did the room change?"

He replied, "The room never changed Kevin, only your perception did. You saw the magic of fear, the lie of fear that binds bondage to ignorance, that at the root of fear is the illusion of oneself obtaining control of their free will when the reality is fear is a weapon of control to remove oneself from their free will."

"These people are in a permanent subconscious headspace of fear and torture but are not aware of it because consciously they are enjoying the pleasures of illusions to appease their selfish desires created by The Door Master's lust for control. You see they trade their consciousness for security. They trade their consciousness, so they don't have to face the reality of their subconscious, the reality of their chains. Their chains that tie them to a world of fear of the unknown all the way down to the core of who they are."

By the time he finished, he had walked up to me and began to lead me towards the altar.

The Narrator continued, "This is the Altar of Fear and this thrown sits The Door Master of The Room of Fear. Please, take a look."

I began to examine the horrific images in front of me as The Door Master was chained to her thrown rocking back and forth. Colorful veins of what seemed to be glowing fluid passed from the thrown and stretched all the way to the crowd of people.

The Narrator looked at the confused look on my face and began to explain. "You see, Kevin, this trance creates fear in the subconscious of all the prisoners and the energy passes to the throne of The Door Master who is also in the same trance, she also is in this reality room in a subconscious state. The Door Master can come in and out of realms whether it's her illusions of beauty or the truth of her lies. She uses this energy to create the beauty you experienced when you first arrived. She uses this energy to make her company compensated for their gift of consciousness in return, while there subconscious is tortured with fear and ignorance. She also uses this energy to create her own beauty and satisfy her personal pleasures in this parallel realm."

I fell to my knees and began to shake I was so cold and confused as everything was so beautiful and now everything was so weird and scary.

"I'm scared," I said to The Narrator.

He responded, "Fear is a part of life, but fear is to be resisted and overcome so the freedom of your mind can expand."

The Door Master looked terrifying. She was practically a skeleton with rotten cartilage covering her body and long white hair. I cannot believe I was so attracted to her. It made my stomach turn. As her beauty, her smell, the expensive ballroom, and the food was nothing more than the product of the subconscious fear of a helpless group of souls. This scared me so much I began to panic, so I took the scope off my eyes and...

WHAM!

I zapped back into the beauty. Even though I knew everything was a lie, at least I could feel the comfort of beauty instead of horror. I decided to justify my decision because I was going to try and convince people to wake up. So I walked around looking for someone that looked easy to talk to and I saw a short nice looking man sitting on a couch.I decided my first plan of action was to go sit next to him on his couch, then convince him this was all a lie.

The couch was made out of silk and he began to say "This couch is so nice, don't you think? I sit here a lot as silk reminds me of my mother. This silk couch was given to me by the goodness of Queen Shanti. She's such a great leader."

I interrupted and said, "Do you really believe this is real? What if there's more than what meets the eye? Would you want to know?"

He responded "Yes, but what more is there than what meets the eye? Does this silk couch not feel like silk and the food not fill your belly? What is more real than what you can touch? Really touching is really all I know to be real, so why question it if there's no way to prove there's more on the other side? "

I began to think about what he was saying. I started feeling like he was persuading me instead of me persuading him. It just made me think of holding my mom and dad, and my sisters again and a tear fell.

He continued "So selfless in her giving and so wealthy she has more than enough to make everyone feel comfortable. That is what you want right? Comfort? You should go before the throne of Queen Shanti and tell her what you want, her goodness surpasses imagination and she will grant you what you want most."

As I approached her thrown, I realized I wanted my mom and dad and to go home. If there was a possibility, I was willing to take the chance. I stepped up the altar and bowed.

She exclaimed, "Come, boy, what is it your heart desires most?"

I replied, "I desire my family can you give me my home back."

I felt guilty for what I was doing. Not consulting The Narrator seems wrong but I couldn't see him, and I hope he can't see me because, at this point, I want to go home regardless. If she could give me my home than I have to try.

She began by saying "I can give you anything you want, but I need you to prick your finger on the end of my dagger and be willing to give a drop of blood."

I remembered what The Narrator had said and remembered the veins of colorful bondage flowing from the subconscious of many to the consciousness of one. I got scared and realized I was about to become a part of the crowd of ignorant souls tortured in a parallel dimension. So, I grabbed my scope and put it to my eyes. Immediately, I saw those big turquoise eyes staring directly into my scope from the other side and he said, "Are you done yet?"

I replied, "Done what?"

"Done playing with this devil witch? You got some nerve, would never sacrifice your reality for comfort in your consciousness?"

I replied, "I want to go home… I don't want to do this."

He said, "Kevin, you're here for a reason and you're not going anywhere 'til you go through the process of facing your battles. This is your dream, your dream that's dying to become a reality. You just have to trust me. If you would have given her your blood you would have fallen into eternity, an eternity you would never return from."

I told him, "This is not what I want. I'm just confused and desperate. Narrator, don't you understand?"

He said softly, "I understand, son, but moving forward is like chopping down a tree, eventually, it's got to fall."

Feeling understood, I responded, "I will do what you ask as it seems to be the only way out without selling my subconscious to a witch and becoming a vegetable without even realizing it. What do you suggest we do, Narrator?"

"I suggest we take off the chains of The Door Master so you can face her in battle."

"Are you crazy! I'm not a warrior! I'm 14 years old!"

He interrupted "Hey, hey, calm down. Do you trust me?"

I replied, "Yes."

He continued, "Okay, follow me. You'll be alright. Follow me not just now, but what's beyond."

So, I followed him up the altar and he unlocked her shackles and a loud screech came from The Door Master as she began to yell "Why have you awoken me from my dwelling place! This is my domain! My consciousness is in my control and I have free will to use it through the illusions I create!"

The Narrator took my hand and started walking towards the door that would take us back to the beautiful hallway. I reached for the handle and I heard the screech again coming from The Door Master and heard a whoosh! When I turned around The Narrator and The Door Master were staring face to face, but The Narrator had a scope of his own between his eyes and The Door Master's eyes.

Then he said to The Door Master, "You may have control of your consciousness, but you make demands as if you have control over me. You know who I am and that I have shown mercy by looking through my scope, so you're not destroyed on contact by seeing my face as it really is. Fortunately for you, your time has not yet come, and your demise will come through me and simultaneously through my warrior."

She rolled her eyes and began laughing walking back to the altar on which she came.

The Narrator continued, "Your powers and strength are an illusion and you know you are weak and frail. One day in years to come you know the prophecy of a warrior destroying you and the power you have over your prisoners will come to pass."

She replied, "You have your plans, Ponyboy, and I have mine. Right now, all you have as your mighty warrior is a scared weak teenager, I will seduce him and make him my slave."

Just like that the door opened and we walked into the hallway and shut the door behind us. I looked at The Narrator and said, "The prophecy? What prophecy?"

He replied as we walked towards another door, "The prophecy of total destruction of evil, Kevin. A warrior that will destroy everything behind these hallway walls. A revolution of the impossible, an anthem for the weak to become strong, growing in numbers an army will form. The warrior will have a special mission of changing the course of history, the history of all the lost souls behind these doors. This man is a complex man and still is waiting on time to bend the origins of his realities."

Wow! What a nice story. I wish he would hurry up because the prophecy is obviously not about me. I'm a boy and he said himself that a man will fulfill the prophecy. I was relieved to know this wasn't my responsibility to get the lost souls out of this mess, battling scary skeletons. I want cookies and milk and a new bike from my dad. That's where my head's at...

He interrupted abruptly, "Timing is order and the order of time is to be determined."

"To be determined?" I thought to myself.

Interesting... I started to think about The Door Master and how she could give me anything I wanted. I started thinking about having dinner with my family, hanging out with my friends at the mall. I began to cry as I remembered all the beauty I once had. I couldn't help but want to take The Door Masters offer.

This "Narrator" guy has my attention, but honestly, I'm afraid to follow him any further, I don't want to go into any other rooms or be a part of any of this weird world I'm in. I'm exhausted from everyone I see. Not that they all scare me or anything, it's just with each new person I meet I realize they are not who I'm really looking for. Every time I see a person in the distance, I hope it's my mom or dad or someone I love. Everything I'm looking for seems so close yet so far away. The uncertainty of not knowing where this road will lead is making me begin to feel desperate.

As my feelings turn into thoughts my thoughts begin to develop a plan. A plan to take The Door Masters deal! A plan to get away from The Narrator! How could I do this? I looked at the door and saw a padlock, however, this padlock was not locked so I could just run through and not say anything. Then again, I don't know what The Narrator is capable of… I need something real, something tangible that I can use as an excuse to go back in. I remembered how scary everything was and began to second guess my plan, but then I remembered that's only when I look through the magical scope.

"THAT'S IT!" I thought to myself.

I'll tell him my scope dropped out of my pockets on the way out! That's good. Wait… that couldn't work. Unless I make it work, of course. I like it, I like this rather well actually.

So, I began my story, "Oh no, Narrator! Your scope! It fell out of my pocket on the way out, I need to get it for the next door."

The Narrator responded saying, "Oh, really? Well, you don't really need it for anything moving forward, that is if you want to move forward?"

"Hmm…" I thought to myself, "If I tell him I want to move forward I'll have no reason to get the scope, and I just can't come up with another reason to go back in or he'll suspect something is going on, and I don't want that to happen."

I replied, "Narrator, listen I miss my family and for the time being, you're all I have, and you gave me this scope. It's special to me. I will get back to my parents at some point and when I do, I want this gift to remind me of you!"

He replied instantly, "A gift. I see, Kevin. Those who need a gift, those who need something tangible to believe or to remember me will never understand me enough to make me worth remembering or understanding… but you have free will, I will be here waiting for you in this hallway while you do what you need to do to get through this dream of yours. Go and do what you set out to do, but remember I asked you to walk with me in the moment we met and also what was beyond that moment. This includes right now, Kevin."

I felt bad and didn't really know what to say to that. What could I say? So, I looked ahead at the Door of Fear and stepped through.

The Surprise:

Chapter 4

I was so excited as I knew she could give me my family. Everyone in the room was so happy. I know their bodies were just being held in place in reality, but really what's the difference? If she will give me exactly what I want I would give my body over to be in an illusion with my family. I see no way out in the place anyway. I don't know how I got here or when or if I will ever be able to go home. I'm confident that an illusion is better than my reality at this point.

As I stepped through the door, I looked around at all the happy people. I assume all these people wanted a rich lifestyle and to be companions with The Door Master in her alternate reality she created for herself. When I shut the door, the beautiful queen or princess was walking towards me, again with such elegance.

She came close and she said, "I see your back so soon, have you decided to join me in this place of unlimited possibilities?"

I replied, "I want my parents, but I don't want them here. I want to go home. I want to return to my life as I knew it before

I came here. I don't want to see you or The Narrator or anyone in this room I just want things to go back to normal, can you give this to me?"

"If your old life is what you want then, yes. I can give you that. Come take my hand and follow me."

She reached out and I grabbed her soft warm hand. She still looked so beautiful despite my knowledge of her real appearance. We started heading towards her altar when I started to feel excited and happy as I knew I was soon to see my family again. I noticed I could hardly breathe from the excitement. It started to make me feel uncomfortable how hard I began gasping for air.

As discomfort turned into panic, I hoped The Narrator was around. I COULDN'T BREATHE! Knowing I never lost my scope I took it out of my pocket and put it to my eyes, hoping to see the narrator.

SNAP!

Immediately everything changed. Not just the appearance of the room this time but I realized I was no longer holding the hand of a beautiful royal girl, but a terrifying skeleton was carrying me by my throat! That's why I couldn't breathe. I gasped words from my mouth saying, "Please put me down!" by the time we got to the altar and she dropped me on the top step near her throne. When I finally caught my breath, I stared at The Door Master still holding the scope to my eyes.

The Door Master began speaking while pulling a dagger from the side of her throne and said, "It's time to bring things back to what you have asked me for, all I need from you is a drop of blood to fall below my feet."

I was afraid but determined to get home, so I took my finger and cut the tip till I saw enough blood to produce a drip. Time stood still and everything went silent as I saw my blood fall to the ground beneath her. When the blood hit the ground, the concrete absorbed my blood creating its own individual colorful vein. This vein was different this vein was moving towards me like a colorful liquid tar it was coming in and out of the concrete like it was alive. I was so terrified I stood to my feet and started walking backwards.

I yelled, "What is this? No! No!"

All I could hear at this point was The Door Master laughing and saying "The deal is done. Now your blood is mine!"

I stepped back so far that I bumped into another prisoner that was in a trance and right then this colorful vein latched onto my foot and I could no longer move. It began to grow up my body covering everything up to the back of my head. At this point, the scope was getting very hard to hold onto. I knew I was going to drop it and right at that moment this colorful vein pierced my eyes, and everything went black. I was still in my head but there was nothing left but thought. As a few seconds past colorful movements of matter formed three separate hallways and at the end of each hallway was like a screen, but different. It was like I could see three moving pictures of real-life quality right in front of me.

I saw my dad chopping wood in one hallway with me mowing the lawn behind him. This was a memory, I realized. This was the time I hit the family of rabbits and my dad was there and made me feel stupid for being overly hysterical because this family of rabbits I killed...

Then in the second hallway, I saw my mother and father and me in a hospital room and my mother was giving birth to my sister Carrie. This was also a memory!

This is not what I signed up for. What have I done! A chill began to go down my spine as I realized why this room was called "The Fear Room." I couldn't close my eyes, I couldn't speak, all I could do was watch my life go by.

I looked down the third hallway and saw my dad holding me in a puddle of blood upstairs in my bedroom. I noticed my grandpa's knife was on the floor next to me. This is strange I thought to myself. I've never been through this, yet it felt oddly familiar. Could this be what happened that caused me to enter into this world? Could I be in hell? Or some type of afterlife? No... no…. I would never do that, plus I have no memory of it anyway. It wouldn't make sense to have to real memories of mine and then a third memory that I have no recollection of.

I saw my dad crying and screaming at his phone, "HURRY! HURRY HIS PULSE IS WEAK! WHAT DO I DO?"

I came to the conclusion this was nothing more than a false scenario just to instill fear in me, as this was the room of fear. I decided to only focus my attention on the two real memories as it gave me some comfort to see my parents and not see myself laying in a puddle of blood.

In the first hallway, I stared at myself walking back and forth mowing the lawn. I started and focused all my attention and the scene it began to get so close to my eyes I began to see through the eyes of my body in this scene and then all the sudden I snapped out of the trance and zapped right back to where my vision could see all three hallways.

I thought to myself, "What was that? Could this be real? Could I relive these memories? Or better yet could I remain in my body and live the rest of my life out?"

Thinking about how I was stuck here and had nothing better to do I decided I would let go. I would surrender and see what happens. I began to stare intently into the picture. I stared at the grass and focused on mowing the lawn. This was a type of experiment to see how far I could take it. I was moving up and down our backyard and my vision got closer and closer.

ZAP!

In front of me I could see the grass. I could feel the nice breeze of the summer air and hear my dad chopping wood. I looked at my dad and there he was, working away! Oh, this felt so good. I never thought I would be so happy as I was at home mowing my yard when all the sudden the lawn mower stalled, and I heard a loud thud!

"NO!" I thought to myself as I remembered the sound.

Surely, I would not do this a second time. I was so distracted by the excitement of being here... being home... I totally forgot to save this family of rabbits the second time around.

I moved the mower to the side and heard my dad's voice say,

"Son, what did you hit?"

As he walked close, I was on my knees watching just like I did the last time. I was looking at mostly dead rabbits and a few babies badly injured. As my dad got close enough to see what happened I heard him say,

"Oh no, son. Poor babies."

I began to cry as I did before, but it was out of confusion and frustration this time. I wanted to change this memory, not repeat it. My dad notices me hysterically crying and said "Son, it's okay. You didn't know!"

As he stood up and told me to close my eyes. I remembered what was next. My dad put the babies out of their misery with the heel of his boot.

THUD! THUD! THUD!

I heard it.

I told my dad, "No! Don't do that we could save them!"

After he was finished, he picked me up to my feet and said "Son, some things you just can't save. Some things you can't change. You had no way of knowing."

I replied, "Yes, but Dad, you don't understand. I could have been more careful! You don't get it!"

He interrupted "Kevin, I don't know what's gotten into you, but this was not your fault. I don't know why you're letting this bother you so much, but you need to grow up! Buck up and realize these kinds of things are out of your control."

I remembered the way I felt the first time around but now I'm starting to make the connection. Up until now, everything that has happened has been the exact same. This time my consciousness is different because I know I'm reliving it. The trouble I'm having with this connection is how my present reality circumstances are producing the same exact results in a predetermined memory that's become my new reality. I have to tell him, I thought to myself. I have to ask him for help! So, as I began to speak. "Dad?"

"Yes, Kevin?"

"I'm tra…."

ZAP!

I was back facing all three hallways!

"Dang it," I thought to myself.

The minute I went off script I came back. I tried five more times different combinations of plans that I thought through the next long while. Each plan I believed in because I had an unlimited amount of time to think. The conclusion I came to is that I can't change the past. I can only relive it.

Carrie:

Chapter 5

Desperate for change, I could no longer relive this memory another time. I changed my focus. I looked at the middle hallway and saw my mom in labor. I was young and I was nervous. I tried to remember what it felt like to be in the room. By this time, I was a pro at getting sucked into my memories.

...and ZAP! I was in!

My mom was screaming as the nurses were frantically pacing around switching her positions as they were waiting on the doctor. I heard the nurses tell my dad that her blood pressure was dangerously high, and they were going to have to go into emergency surgery to get my sister out safely. I ran to my mom and hugged her. I was scared the first time I lived this, but this time I wasn't scared as I knew she would be okay. I just wanted to hold her again.

"Mom, I love you so much"

She replied, "I love you too, baby. Everything's going to be okay."

"I know it will," I said.

Everything was the same just my perception had changed.

My dad looked at me as they wheeled my mom into another room and said, "Kevin everything's going to be okay, but you're going to have to wait in the lobby while I go with your mom."

I replied, "Okay, but Dad, can I hug Mom again? I don't want her to leave! I miss her!"

I started to cry, just as I did the first time.

"Yes," he said, "but we have to hurry!"

My dad picked me up as I was just a little boy and ran to my mom's bed in the hallway as the nurses were rushing her to the surgery room and put me on her chest.

The nurse said, "Sorry, sir. But you can't do that!"

As my dad began to pull me away from my mom, my mom held onto my hands tightly and said "Everything's okay, honey. I'll see you soon. I love you…"

My dad took me into the lobby and said "Wait right here, son. I'll come get you when your sister is born."

Ahh… the long wait. I remember this part. This time it was different because I knew my mom was going to be okay, but it felt like a lifetime since I had seen her.

The first time I lived this waiting period out I was afraid she was going to die and I was alone. I never knew how much this memory impacted me 'til I relived it from a different perception. This is so strange.

I waited for a long 30 minutes when my dad came and said, "Kevin are you ready to see Carrie?"

I thought to myself, "Carrie!" I almost forgot!

"Yes, Dad!" I said as I ran towards him.

We walked into the room and my beautiful mom was holding my sister and looked at me and said, "Son, come see your baby sister."

My dad put me on my mom's bed and I almost forgot about my mom as I stared at Carrie. I was so used to her being a little girl, it was amazing to see her as a baby again.

I started crying and said, "Mom, I'm afraid I'm going to lose you."

She replied, "Kevin, I know this was scary for you, but everything's okay."

I know I can't go off the script at this point and she just doesn't understand. Everything that was said was exactly the same as the first time I lived through this. What an amazing experience I took for granted. I mean, I never knew that I would disappear into another world, but I can really take it all in now. I felt more alive now than ever. I held my mom as we watched cartoons.

"Daddy, can I have soda, please?"

I remember the few times I drank my favorite drink, "Root Beer," as my mom only let me have it on special occasions. This was one of them.

He responded "You have to ask your mom, kid. You know how she is about sugar..."

My mom said, "Abraham, it's ok. Get your boy a soda."

My dad smiled and said he would be back. When he left, I thought… no, I desired that I could go off script. So, I tried.

"Mom, there's something I need to tell you…"

Right then, ZAP!

I came back to my vision of the three hallways. Woah! That was amazing. I went through this memory dozens of times as it was so pleasant. I began to feel rejuvenated. I was hungry for more of my family, so I went back, and I went back, and I went back… until it began to feel fake.

I didn't know what to do now. I stared at the three hallways and decided I would not go into the last one as it terrified me.

"NO WAY!" I thought to myself.

I don't even know what that scene is. I never got hurt like that in my life. So I began to relive the first hallway memory over and over and when I came back I would consider more and more about going into the third hallway, as this was becoming a torment. I felt I had been here for an eternity.

This pain and fear has drowned me over and over I feel numb and I don't know what's real and what's not real anymore. I'm afraid of myself, I'm afraid of these hallways. I'm scared I'm going insane.

"I've gotta get outta here." I thought to myself.

Over and over again I went to past experiences that I was comfortable with because they made me feel certain. They made me feel protected and secure until finally, I looked at my biggest fear head on out of desperation. I looked at the third hallway down the middle and imagined what it would be like in that puddle of blood and…
ZAP!

I became one with this unknown and very scary scene.

The Last Straw:

Chapter 6

Nothing.

Darkness was all I could see. I could hear my dad screaming and I could feel him holding me close. He whispered in my ear as I began to hear sirens in the background.

"Son, I'm so sorry. Everything will be okay… I got you! I won't let anything happen to you again, just keep fighting! Stay with me!"

I heard the sound of the front door slam and several people shuffle up the stairs.

"Is he breathing?" I heard a strange voice ask.

"Yes," my dad replied. "but I can barely feel his pulse!"

I felt hands all over me putting pressure on my arm. Wrapping a cuff around my arm. "Okay, Sir. We are going to pick him up and take him to the truck downstairs. Let's move fast!"

I felt arms around me picking me up into a cradle position. Then I was set on a table. I could see my dad's blurry face.

"Daddy," I said.

"Yes, son? I'm here. Stay with me."

My dad rode in this truck as I heard the sirens and the engine roar off our driveway. When we hurried into the hospital I could barely see and I could hear my heartbeat in my ears. I knew I was about to die.

As my vision went dark, I heard a voice say "His blood pressure is dropping!"

It went black for a second. The next thing I saw was a monitor in my room flatlined and then it began to move... I looked around and saw my mom in the window balling and doctors all around me. I hear them say his blood pressure is dropping again, we need to hit him a second time. It went black again.

Then again, I saw doctors and nurses saying, "He's dropping again. I think we're losing him."

I faded out and heard, "1 2 3 CLEAR!"

...and ZAP!

I came back to see The Narrators face with sparkle-like-diamond liquid on his face. He was ripping the colorful veins from all over my body.

When I was free, he looked into my eyes and said, "Are you ready to move forward?"

I replied, "Oh my God, yes! It's so good to see you!"

Then he said in a soft voice, "Let's get out of here now."

Redemption:

Chapter 7

-The second level of understanding the preface-

As I stare into my canvas, I see how each brush stroke makes such a difference. Every time I change my mind on the direction, I realize that every stroke has a specific purpose, a place in the overall painting. For the greater good, I should say. What if I randomly splatter a pointless stroke of disaster? Another way I could look at this question is, could this be nothing more than a stroke of luck? Oh, that's good. Wait, that couldn't work unless I make it work of course. Interesting concept, I like this concept rather well actually.

See, we all have these expectations in life, these "labeled boxes" that we put our personal experiences in. What a beautiful picture of how we all play a personal role, a personal part in this story we call life. The proof is, we do all have different expectations don't we? Great! We agree on this matter then. This reminds me of my whole point. Humanity, please bear with me, as I know we're all tired of the cliché philosophical RA-RA that were unbelievably used to in life. However, humanity is all we as a race seem to understand on a surface level. Perhaps, our perception of humanity is only a figment of your imagination. I feel the word "imagination" comes across too colorful in this context. I think "desire" may better express what I mean. A "desire" to better understand ourselves as humans is what we all simultaneously are trying to accomplish.

This brings me to my secondary point. See, I think... no, I "desire" that there is more to the human race than what meets the naked eye. Lastly, My tri-angular point in the opening of this book, or maybe it's more of an offer to you as the individual reader. Follow me into my dream, my masterpiece painting of a canvas. Literally, with your heart's permission, I will take you on a journey to the center of the canvas. This canvas is you. This canvas is me. Your life is the strokes of the brush that provide the color of your life. Your life that we think of as our "personal" experiences. Be warned! Don't get lost or lose your way as this is an artistic journey. Try and keep up to not only to what the tri-eye can see, but what is beyond deep, deep into the subconscious of what you "perceive" as the human race. Still, as humanity remains a singular consciousness, yet separated by personal but very unique energetic entities. This is exactly as strange as you "perceive" this to be. Still, I ask to follow me into the colorful life of a boy named Kevin.

The Narrator took my hand as we walked out of the room of fear. I was so relieved. I noticed on our way out that The Witch was in her throne in a trance as was everyone else.

We opened the door and stepped through into the hallway. I heard the door latch and I stretched out my arms around the narrator and he put his arms around me. He held me.

So many times, I went through those memories in The Fear Room and my dad held me over and over. It was so comforting, but nothing like this. Nothing like what I have found in The Narrator. At this point, I was as happy to see him as I was my mom and my dad. He was strong but gentle. I felt thankful but extremely guilty for what I had done.

"I'm so sorry, Narrator. Could you forgive me?"

He responded "My forgiveness is far greater than any mistake. Mistakes are the cause of forgiveness, yet they are separated by one thing, me... I separate the two. Mistakes are like dead leaves falling from a tree in the fall and my forgiveness is the life that causes new leaves to grow in the spring. I am the tree that is there through it all separating season from season. Do you understand? My forgiveness cannot be compared to any mistake. As mistakes pass, just like the seasons. My forgiveness is a part of who I am as the tree and I will always remain."

I was crying at this point and I broke down. He wasn't even mad at me. I started to confide in him like I would my dad back home.

I started by saying, "Narrator, I lied to you about the scope. It was all a lie. I wanted to see my family again, but I was deceived into thinking it was possible to go home. I'm not blaming anyone. It was my choice.

"However, I didn't get to go home, I was forced to live in the past. I relived the same memories over and over.

"There was one thing I went through that I didn't understand. See, everything was memories of the past except one. I was in a puddle of blood and I almost died. When I went to the hospital, they shocked me three times and on the 3rd time, you came for me. What do I make of this?"

He responded "Kevin, what you experienced is a mystery and some mysteries can only be understood through experience. You are equipped to face the future in front of you, no matter what it is. You're stronger than you think. Life will come at you with unexpected information that can produce all kinds of emotions. Emotions can lead to drastic mistakes. However, mistakes lead to my forgiveness and my forgiveness leads to your purpose in this life and beyond.

"Take control over your emotions, Kevin. You go through pain because it's making you who you're supposed to be. Your mission has not even begun. You have many purposes.

"There is purpose in everything. When you're ready, you will know and nothing will stop you.

"You decide when you're ready. The unknown is a tool that creates circumstances to train you to trust me. Train you to understand that I don't give you guidelines because I am on some kind of power trip, but because I have a plan to make you strong through the process. I lead you and inform you on what to do because I want to protect you from pain. Although free will and evil people hurting you will always be a problem until evil is uprooted once in for all, I will allow the free will of evil people and your mistakes to shape you in the process."

I started thinking to myself, "This is so much to take in."

I wasn't sure who The Narrator was entirely, but I knew he

seemed to care about me and everyone. When he spoke to me, he spoke to me personally, at the same time he spoke in a way that made it clear he feels the same way towards everyone.

"Thank you, Narrator, for saving me from The Fear Room."

He responded, "I'll always be here for you Kevin. Now the time has come. Are you ready to face your battles?"

I was drained... I mentally took a few moments to pull myself together and then I responded "Yes, I'm ready... what door do we go through next?"

The Root of Everything:

Chapter 8

We were standing in front of the next door and more chills went down my spine. As I continued to observe, I saw a door that had a wooden plate that read, "The Trauma Room."

This sign was amazing! The person who made this sign spent an insane amount of time on it. The maker made each letter out of rows of screws, so close together it looked as if it was a single letter. Row by row made each letter that spelled out "The Trauma Room."

The sign made me uncomfortable, so I asked, "You want me to go into this 'Trauma Room?'"

He responded, "Kevin, this is your dream, your dream that's dying to become a reality.

This is also your trauma room. You play a specific role, for a specific purpose with what's beyond this door. There will be a Door Master with no name. He will think he knows what your role is, but only you can decide what your role is.

"In this room and all the other rooms to come after we go our separate ways, never forget, even though you will step in by yourself, you will not be alone. I will always be with you. Through the pain, through the fear, through the anxiety. All of these trials serve a purpose and will make you who you were created to be. You have the ability to overcome this room and come out unscratched physically.

"I give my word, and my word is as real as my flesh. If you ever get to a place where you lose hope and you can't go any further just call my name three times and I'll instantaneously be there."

Right as The Narrator said those words, I turned around, and he was gone. It made me sad that he just disappeared.

I wasn't ready to do this, I thought to myself.

I took a couple of steps back and stared at this door for about seven minutes and I reached for the doorknob and thought to myself, "Here goes nothing, or something I don't know which witch is which anymore."

A twist of the glowing knob and I stepped through.

As I stepped into this room the first thing that I noticed was, well, nothing. This wasn't traumatic, like the sign lead me to believe, but I remember what The Narrator said.

"Perception is what makes my reality real."

So, I proceeded with caution. I couldn't tell which way I was walking, only that I was walking. Then, I remembered the torch outside the door and thought it would be nice to have. So, I turned around, and right as I turned, I noticed the door was gone.

A bright light appeared in my peripheral. Instantly, I felt comfort. The kind of comfort I felt from my mother when she would hold me in her arms when I was a child.

"I have to find out where this light was coming from." I thought.

When I turned around, expecting to find this comforting light. I instead saw a man standing there, an extremely large man.

This couldn't be a man. He had to be eight feet tall. He made my Dad look like a leprechaun with his biceps the size of my head and veins popping out in every direction possible.

He was wearing all black silk. His shirt was like a button up vest made out of silk. But not just any silk, it was like some advanced technologically produced armor. His pants were made out of the same material, just black silk-like armor, and his feet were fitted with something like black combat boots from my "perception."

This word "Perception," started to stand out more and more in my mind. I was beginning to understand deeper levels of this word.

"Whoosh!" was the next sound I heard, as I saw the giant swing a hammer towards my arm. This scared the living gems out of me as I thought this hammer would surely end my life.

"Smack!"

I heard as I felt this metal strap around my wrist close tightly.

I looked down my arm and saw an old-fashioned cuff with a bolt through it. That's what the hammers job was. To put this bolt through this rustic cuff with what looked like dried blood all over it.

This cuff on my wrist was connected to a chain which was also connected to another cuff on this giant man's wrist, which when I looked further, I saw his other wrist also had a cuff on it with a chain. This chain was long... very long, but I couldn't quite seem to find where this chain was leading.

I sort of put two and two together and figured out this was what The Narrator was trying to explain when he said there would be a Door Master waiting for me. I began to realize the gravity of the choice I made, stepping into this room, as I began to feel traumatized by what was occurring before my own eyes.

At the same time, I felt comforted by this pure glow of a light that allowed my eyes to see in the first place. Something inside was hoping The Narrator was nearby, shining some expensive spotlight in the room somewhere. Since I couldn't hear his voice or see his huge turquoise eyes, I began to feel very scared.

Very afraid of this room. I started to panic and then, just then I saw the light, or at least what was the source of this beautiful light. It was a surprisingly unique dancer. Just dancing with no music, she clearly didn't need any music. Gliding through the air it soared one step after another, in a floating fashion. Each step landed on the top of what appeared to be cubicles.

The best way I can describe it is like cubicles in an office building. What I'm saying is best explained through telemarketing cubicles with walls about five feet tall. With each beautiful step she made, on the top of each cubicle wall, I saw a glimpse of a person in each cubicle along the way. I couldn't see much of these people's characters, only that they were there.

The Door Master with no name then said, "Follow me, soul."

This choice of words sent a chill down my spine that surpassed all the beauty that flowed from the light.

I spiraled out of control in my racing thoughts, and began to yell, "LET ME OUT! LET ME OUT OF THESE CHAINS. I DON'T BELONG IN THIS ROOM!"

The Door Master gave one swift move of his huge arm and

I flew three feet forward. I realized The Narrator was wrong... There was no getting out of this room. The door was gone, and the door that no longer existed was guarded by a very powerful and authoritative character.

He seemed to have no emotion. No remorse for the way he was making me feel. I was broken. I was numbed by the situation and began to comply. He picked me up by the throat and gently set me to my feet looking directly into my eyes. I noticed his helmet had a black titanium piece of metal covering both eyes.

I thought to myself, "I don't think he can see me. I know I can see him."

I remembered what The Narrator had told me, "The eyes are the window to the soul."

All I could see of his soul was a black darkness. Just... nothing. I almost had pity on him because as I looked into his eyes that could not see, he too was in chains.

He led the way, beginning to walk through a tiny, very small hallway. A hallway through all these cubicles. I "chose" no I "desired" to follow with no resistance, despite the pain I was experiencing.

We came to the first cubicle with another huge man inside. Now this man was very human. A reasonably sized giant with bulging muscles. He was pacing back and forth looking like Captain America with his hands on his cheeks rubbing his face back and forth. He had scabs and sores on his face obviously from rubbing his face raw.

I was afraid of him as well. Then, I saw a shift in the light provided by this beautiful dancer, as she jumped in a Matrix-style way and landed right in front of The Door Master.

Like I said, I don't think he can see. It's almost like some sort of dark energy just pulls him from one place to another like a zombie.

This dancer, with a beautiful, form-fitting gown, started to burst out in elegant expressive dancing around The Door Master. In her dancing, she leans over and blows with a hard airflow to his forehead. Right in the middle of his forehead, almost like she blew into the front part of his brain.

I remember this part of the brain from seventh grade science class. It was a strange topic about some kind of molecule or something, maybe a hormone? Anyway, I don't know, I just remember the acronym DMT. I remember learning how it was what produced our dreams, and also where near death experiences came from. It seemed like, right when the dancer breathed into this holding place of The Door Master's DMT, he began to be controlled by her. Almost as if this dancer could manipulate his actions.

Suddenly, he turned to me and said, "Talk to my prisoner."

Just as he finished his sentence, the dancer began twirling and spinning across the hallway and jumped so high I would have thought she would have gone through the roof.

When I looked up, I noticed there wasn't any roof that existed. A foggy darkness was all I could see above me. Still, as far high up in the air as this dancer went her light shone down on me, now sitting on the cold concrete floor next to this "prisoner".

I looked across the hall and noticed another prisoner inside of his cubicle, outraged and just screaming, clawing at me. But thank God he could not get near me because he too was bound by his chains.

I looked to my left and I could see for miles, just cubicle after cubicle. I realized this chain was actually nothing more than a train of prisoners. At the head of this train was The Door Master, who was also bound by his chains. That screaming man in his cubicle was drooling all over his face. I saw patches of hair missing from his head.

He was just screaming, "Let me out or I'll kill you!! I'll eat your flesh if you don't let me out!"

"Screeching" is really the best descriptive word I can come up with for this man's voice. The large man in the other cubicle I was in front of was still rubbing his face, and now, I felt more comfortable sitting next to him after looking at the drooling maniac across the hall.

This rather large man starts by saying to me, "Don't mind him, he never stops. He only repeats himself over and over and over. I've tried talking to him and it never goes anywhere."

I responded, "I see, and who are you?"

"My name is Greg," and he reached over and hugged me.
In my mind, I was a little grossed out by the scabs that were now rubbing against my face. He seemed so gentle despite his

size. I knew he meant me no harm now.

"What is this place we're in Greg? Where are we?"

He responded, "Hell if I know, kid. All I know is I've been here ever since I can remember, and I don't remember anything since I've been here. The only things I remember, I've put into paintings all around us."

I then began to look around his cubicle and I saw art piece after art piece, picture after picture of very disturbing images. One picture in particular was of a little boy being raped.

In quotations at the top of the picture it read, "You were my father, how could you rape me?"

Other pictures were not so offensive, like the pictures of him shooting up steroids. Each picture of him shooting up his body mass grew bigger and bigger. He had dozens of pictures of him working out, with quotations at the top of each picture reading, "Am I a man yet, Dad?"

So, I asked him, "What's with all these paintings?"

He then started his dialogue, "My wife left me. I tried telling her about my P.T.S.D., about how my father raped me on my seventh birthday. He was supposed to take me to Legoland and have a boys' night at a hotel just me and my dad. How naive of me.

"Anyway, my wife couldn't handle my drug usage and all the fights that came along with all my pain. I'm a good father. It's about the only thing I'm good at. My daughters love me so much. I take them out every chance I get. I'm just stuck in my childhood and embarrassed over being raped by a man, let alone my father. This makes me feel dirty and used. I try to be as tough and as strong as a man is supposed to be in my eyes. I can prove to others and myself that I am a man, right? I am a man now, right kid?"

Just as he finished his story the beautiful dancer came into the cubicle and started doing her thing, dancing in the middle of us.

Greg seemed to be unaware of her presence, but I was not only aware but again in awe.

Her dancing was always new. New spins, new hand movements and stretching in such an artistic way. She made her way over towards me.

Since I knew she comes and goes so fast, I didn't want her to leave me. I grabbed onto her white gown in fear and instantly the fear left. I was going to beg her to get me out of here but now I had a change of heart. I know why I'm here. I'm here for Greg.

As she glided back up through the roof that didn't exist and as her light shone down on me from above, I began to heal Greg. I was standing face to face with Greg and without hesitation, I put both of my golden hands on his scabby face and commanded him to look into my eyes, as the eyes are "the window to the soul."

I thought to myself, "Let the healing begin."

I told Greg with authority, "Greg, you were a boy and I'm sorry for what happened to you. I want you to look into my eyes so I can speak to your soul."

He submitted to me, this little boy, right? This boy that was half the size as him. For a second I could see him as a boy and I said, "Greg... Greg... this wasn't your fault. You did not ask for that to happen to you. Your dad was wrong. You are a man. Look at yourself Greg you look great. You're handsome, you have a body that reminds me of Hercules." He let out a halfway chuckle with a smile on his face.

I then told him, "Your body isn't the issue, so keep working on your body and stay healthy. The point is, Greg, don't let your body decide whether or not you're a man. You're a man because you're a man, and you prove that by loving your wife and your children. That's who you are."

I felt an amazing lift from his spirit. He looked well. His scabs were gone and as a smile overtook his face, his shackles broke free from his wrist and he began to dance. Not so elegant like the beautiful dancing I'm used to at this point, but that was enough for me. He was dancing out of his cubicle, and before I knew it, I couldn't see him. I didn't see him leave the room, only dance away and disappear into the distance.

When I looked down at his broken shackles, I looked at mine in hoping mine too were broken. With sadness, I felt another tug that pulled my legs out from underneath me and I dropped on my chest by this annoyingly strong Door Master. The Door Master started dragging me down the narrow hallway of these terrified people. Again the beautiful dancer appeared, and again she blew air directly at The Door Master's forehead.

He stopped and said, "Talk to this prisoner, soul!"

The House Fire:

Chapter 9

After The Door Master picked me up and pushed me into another cubicle. Since I knew how the last encounter with a prisoner played out, I was expecting to help someone else, with instructions from the dancer. When I came to the next cubicle there was a beautiful girl, a little younger than me.

I asked her, "How old are you?"

She said, "I'm 12 years old," next she asked me, "How old are you?"

"I'm 14," I replied.

"It's nice to meet you," we both said.

She was sitting on the ground, sitting crisscross applesauce. She looked like she had been crying for some time. I couldn't help but fall in love with who she was. I could see she was naive but also pure and beautiful. I could tell she had been through a lot.

I looked around and again I saw painting after painting and picture after picture. Very disturbed, my heart broke for this girl as I saw this painting of an old wooden house on fire.

In the picture, I saw land around the house. On the land was sitting three boys, one girl and their father crying, staring at their burning house.

On the second story of the house, I saw several little girls passed out from the smoke. These girls were in a circle holding each other, all of their bodies were limp. In the bedroom, there was a window and this window was broken. Out of the broken window, I saw a girl jumping out with blood pouring out of her leg. There were other pictures of several girls' skeletons entwined with each other. Holding each other in the same circle from the first painting.

The caption at the top of the picture read, "I'm sorry I jumped before you, my dear sisters."

I asked her, "What's your name?"

She replied, "My name is Bernette".

I continued, "Do you know where we are, Bernette?"

"No, all I know is I've been here ever since I can remember and I can't remember anything since I've been here." She said in a discouraged voice.

Still influenced by my experience with Greg, I knew why I was here. When I thought back on what The Narrator said to me, I remembered he said that I would get out unscratched. It made me feel like it was possible to get out after I help these people. Maybe I might break free, free of my shackles. That makes sense and I began to respect The Narrator for leaving me such an important task.

"Let the healing begin," I thought to myself.

"Bernette, would you like to tell me about your paintings?"

"Yes," she exclaimed, "I was just in a house fire and it happened so fast. I have a big family. I mean... I had a big family. We were all sleeping. Just before the sun had risen over the horizon, I was woken up by thick black smoke.

"Our house was an old wooden farmhouse with no nearby firefighters. My older sister Maggie came and dragged me into my little sisters' room. All my sisters were terrified, as I was. My older sister Maggie said she would jump first and we would follow. That was the rushed plan we had. My eldest sister broke the window with a nearby chair and jumped. I looked down and she was waiting for me to jump. I had a few older sisters in the room and figured they would help the younger ones get out. I looked back and they were all waiting to get out, so I jumped.

"When I jumped, I made a deep wound on my leg by cutting my thigh on a piece of what was left of my sisters' bedroom window.

"Then, nothing. Just nothing. Nothing happened until I saw my mom's leg come out of her bedroom window.

I thought 'Thank God. Here comes my mommy.'

"Nothing, just nothing. I stared and saw beautiful mom's leg go limp. She passed out from the smoke, as did my sisters.

"When the firefighters finally got there, they put out the fire enough to rush inside to get to my sisters. Nearly just as fast as they went in, they came out, crying hysterically. They were all so traumatized by the skeletons they found in my sisters' room."

When she finished telling me her story, she began to cry and fell into my arms.

While I was holding this poor girl, I looked across the hallway and I could see three cubicles with one firefighter in each cubicle.

They were smashing their heads against the wall, saying "WHY! WHY COULDN'T I SAVE YOU!"

They too had painting after painting of the little girls' skeletons all around them in each of the cubicles of each firefighter. The quotations on top of each painting read "I could have saved you, baby girls. I should have done more."

This broke my heart and I took her by the face and told her, "Look into my eyes."

She interrupted my soul talk I was about to have by saying "Your eyes… your eyes are so beautiful; I've never seen turquoise eyes in my life."

"Turquoise eyes?" I thought.

My eyes are clearly dark brown. She must not be seeing clearly through her tears.

As I held her by the face I said, "I'm sorry, Bernette, for what happened. Sometimes tragedy strikes and no one knows how such bad things can happen for no reason that we can see.

"A wise man once told me there was a bigger picture that made all the hard strokes of life make sense. There was a specific purpose and reason for even the hardest things in life that we cannot understand. This was not your fault. You did not start the fire. It was an accident. You're not responsible for the loss of your loved ones despite all the pain you're going through. You feel like you could have done more is only living in the past and you giving up on your life is only avoiding your future. If you could have done more, you would have. You were forced into a situation where you acted on impulse and you thought they would have made it out after you jumped. I'm sorry, but now you're free, child. This is not your fault."

She was crying a lot at this point and then started dancing as her shackles broke free and she kissed my cheek and danced into the distance. Still not quite as good as the dancing I was used to by the beautiful glowing light, but she came close... so close. Her dancing was so beautiful and struck me deep.

I screamed "Wait! Wait! I want to be with you forever!"

She looked at me and yelled back, "One day, turquoise boy, we shall find each other in another life!"

While I was crying for this girl's presence in my life, I continued to be thrown forward by this dreadfully strong Door Master.

He said, "Come, soul boy. You're mine."

My wrist hurt so bad, I knew I was bleeding, I now knew where the dried blood came from. All the previous prisons entrance to this dreadful dungeon.

When I looked down, I noticed somehow these cuffs never left a scratch. The Narrator's promise so far had been kept. He continued leading me forward. Again the beautiful glowing dancer appeared, and right as she was about to start the "air blowing" thing, I grabbed her hand.

"Please take me with you! Take me away from this! Let me be free," I said.

She turned around and kissed my forehead. A rush of strength filled me up like my carvings filled up my wooden chest back home. She finished her work with The Door Master as she went back through the roof that did not exist.

Suddenly, The Door Master stopped and began to say, "Talk to my..."

I interrupted with a sarcastic attitude and said, "Talk to your prisoner. I know, I know."

This time I walked straight up to the next girl and blatantly asked, "Will you tell me your name?"

She said, "Gabrielle," and next said, "Can I tell you about my paintings?"

"Well, that was easy." I thought, "That's exactly what I wanted to get to."

She started her story saying, "You see these paintings?"

She pointed out four identical paintings.

"I had a surgery where they implanted a medical device in my stomach. This was only supposed to remain in my body for six months. Look at my paintings, I went through four surgeries to get this taken out. They can't take it out. At any time this device can come apart and kill me. Each surgery I have there is an 80% chance of fatality and I made it through every surgery somehow. The problem is, this device has made its way into a main artery, and they can't get it out. If they force it out it will kill me almost instantly. My husband and friends have all been crying for me and my situation."

She then grabbed me by my face and said, "Let me see into your turquoise eyes. Your eyes are speaking to me."

"God's got me," she said, "God's got me".

Instantly, her shackles were broken, and I walked away confused as she began to dance free. I thought I was here to heal her, but it seems she healed herself.

Confused, I started to walk fast before The Door Master had the chance to jerk me around. We walked for what seemed to be miles and I saw all kinds of suffering people with paintings in their holding place. Some I thought I could help, and some seemed terrifying, they seemed more likely that they would kill anyone who got into an arm's reach. Finally, we got to the end of the aisle. I noticed The Door Master turn around and stuck his huge palm in my face.

"Stop," he said.

I was looking for the next individual I was supposed to heal when I heard the sound of the hammer swing towards my cuff lock. I looked down and saw the cuff of The Door Master was now cuffed to a metal "C" clamp on the right side of this cubicle I was now in.

This cubicle was the last holding place in this hallway. Quickly, he snapped another cuff on the other side of the cubicle and I started to panic again now that both my hands were chained, one on each side of this cubicle. I had about six feet of loose chains to move around with. He looked into my eyes, which made me close my eyes tightly. I didn't want him to see. I didn't want him to see what I still believed to be dark brown eyes, not turquoise eyes like I've been told lately.

He then said in a horrible voice, "This is your new soul

home, soul boy."

He walked away. I noticed The Door Master had one cuff on his wrist still that was connected to my cuff by a chain which was connected to all the other prisoners in this room.

All the prisoners were screaming in terror, "LET ME OUT!" I also began to follow their lead screaming in terror.

The Door Master walked away slowly with his head down, dragging behind him a very heavy and very long chain, the chain that connected all of us prisoners behind him.

My New Home:

Chapter 10

I can't believe this. I can't accept where my new home is. I'm so angry. I'm angry with myself, I'm angry with The Door Master and I'm angry with… Oh my God, that stupid Narrator! He's the cause of all of this! I can't believe the Narrator allowed me to get myself into this situation after I confided in him, I trusted him!

I know I made my mistakes and he talked about forgiveness and how he was a tree that doesn't change. His forgiveness cannot be compared to any mistakes. This time he made a mistake by leaving me alone through this door.I can't help but feel anger towards those turquoise eyes that has allowed me to be put me in chains.

Those eyes that once looked into my soul and asked, "Is your knife not the same as my brush and your wooden objects not the same as my canvas?"

"His canvas is me? What a load of crap." I thought to myself.

I'm bound by these chains in a chilling room, and it's full of people who scare me. I know they have all been through trauma. That sucks for them, but I was fine before this.

This is the only trauma I'm going through or have ever gone through. It is this room, this Trauma Room. I don't belong here. While I had this train of thoughts running on the railroads of my mind, I began to look around. Again I saw painting after painting and art piece after art piece. Then my vision went black.

Then ZAP!

I was back in an instant. When my eyes opened again, I had to put the pieces back together. I realized I had just fainted. I stood up and I felt the heavy shackles and saw all the paintings and realized why I blacked out. The first painting I saw wasn't really a painting, it was more of a letter.

The words on this letter read, "All I know is I've been here ever since I can remember and I can't remember anything since I've been here."

That was strange, I could recall almost everyone in this Trauma Room repeating this same line. What chilling words to read from my own personal handwriting. At the same time, not having any recollection of writing this letter, I suddenly blacked out again.

When I came to again, it scared me, thinking that I would never be free. Then, I remembered how I broke the shackles of three people within this door. I hoped for the beautiful dancer. I hoped someone would do the same for me. I saw the next painting. I examined this picture and became terrified at my painting. It was a painting of me cutting my arm with my grandpa's heirloom knife.

The caption at the top of the page read, "You were my world, now my world is over, my daddy and mommy".

This was confusing, this seems like some stalker knew what my room looked like, and painted this fake picture. I remembered the unknown scene from The Fear Room. I would never cut myself. I love my life. I love my mom, my dad, and my sisters.

I then looked at the next picture. It was a picture of me throwing my carving of a family of rabbits at my dad.

The caption read, "How could you be getting a divorce!"

Darkness once again stole my vision away from me and I fainted a third time. When I awoke I gathered my senses and studied the last painting. This painting was really good, like a masterpiece painting, painted by a master artist. This painting was a picture of paramedics tending my wound.

The caption read, "This isn't over 'til I say it's over. I'm with you through it all."

I began to think I was dead. I couldn't help but be comforted by this painting. Thank God I didn't pass out a fourth time, it may have been my last.

Where am I? Why have I been entertaining such a strange phenomenon without question? The Narrator, who I'm extremely angry with. The beautiful dancer, that I would love to see again. The Door Master, who I don't ever want to see again. The businessman Tusk, who I don't know well yet, but still I wonder if he can help me. Where did all these people come from? How did they come into my life? Nothing, just nothing. I couldn't remember anything.

"All I know is I've been here ever since I could remember and I don't remember anything since I've been here."

How strange that I naturally had this thought.

All of a sudden, before my own eyes, I saw the first painting of the letter being brought to life through my thoughts. Still, though, this must be a bad dream, a nightmare or something. I started to want to wake up. I tried everything. Pinching myself. I tried banging my head against the wall. Nothing worked, and right then I saw my heirloom knife on the table.

"If I kill myself in a dream it should wake me up," I thought.

"This has to be a dream. A roof with no roof? A Trauma Room guarded by a Door Master? Precious stones in a multi-dimensional hallway?"

I just wanted out of this situation. This was a desperate move. This move was a cry for attention. This move was planned. This is a dream, so here goes nothing.

As I picked up my knife, I was staring at my arm. Touching this knife changed my surroundings and brought me back into my bedroom. It brought me inside this painting in my cubicle. I never noticed my surroundings change into my bedroom until I cut myself in a horizontal motion and started bleeding.

Just as I noticed I was dying in my own room, I zapped back into my cubicle. In my peripheral vision, I saw the painting and realized I just fulfilled the second picture and started to see these pictures as prophetic.

Now I just need to wait for the paramedics to get me out of here, but after six horrific hours, the paramedics never came. Six horrific hours went by.

I started to think, "Maybe I'm not in a dream and I really just messed up."

Six hours. Each hour I thought, "I don't want to die!"

I started acting like the crazier people in the room, screeching out in fear and slamming my chains forward against my cubicle wall, trying to desperately break free. I noticed I was bleeding from the cut, but it just continued without any effect. So much for "coming out unscratched physically."

I sat down and gave up. As I sat there traumatized, I remembered what The Narrator said.

"If I ever can't go any further, just call his name three times, and he will be there instantaneously."

Excited, I stood to my feet not knowing why I didn't think of this before. Just as I screamed out for The Narrator, for the first time, a glowing flood of pure white came down so fast, it blinded my eyes pushed me to face the ground, bowing before the dancer.

It happened just as instantaneously as The Narrator would have shown up. I never got to finish calling out to The Narrator, but I was okay with that.

Now that the beautiful dancer was twirling right in front of my eyes. I was pissed at The Narrator anyway, to be honest. My pride would much rather get help from this beautiful separate entity dancing around my chains. She was different than The Narrator, yet they both comforted me. She doesn't talk, she just moves powerfully but smoothly. I liked that.

The dancer took my hands and began to pull me forward. Right as I stepped in close, I could feel how powerful she was, despite her little figure. She picked me up like I was a newborn baby and cradled me. She spun around so fast I didn't even notice my shackles break free. She just kept spinning and twirling. She set me down on my feet then and stared into my eyes. Finally, I get to look at this beautiful dancer in the eyes. I noticed she too had huge turquoise eyes.

"What is up with this recurring color turquoise?" I thought to myself.

She hugged me as we swayed back and forth. She stopped moving and put her hands flat in front of my face. While still continuing to look into my eyes, she just held her hands out and I began to think she "desired" for me to mimic her so I began experimenting. I put my hands flat out directly out in front of her flat hands. I started to mirror her, and she smiled and began to move her hands in a circular motion, as I did.

I decided to follow her lead, she does lead so well. Then, she took one slow step to the side as I followed. With a twirl, I began to dance with this glowing spirit. We found our groove as a routine began to form. We moved faster and faster with more and more passion. I felt it. I felt the beauty that this dancer lived in. Instantly, she did this Matrix-style jump and landed on top of my cubicle.

"I can't jump that high," I thought to myself.

She stared at me and waited. I was afraid and looked down. As I looked down, I expected a puddle of blood, but when I looked at my arm it was completely healed. Not one physical scratch. Also, my shackles were now free.

I thought to myself, okay… this is getting interesting, so here goes nothing or something. I don't know which witch is which any more than I did before I stepped through the Trauma Room Door."

I squatted down, preparing to take my leap of faith, and I jumped! It was like the opposite of gravity. As what goes up must come down, but this time I went up higher than the human body can manage.

"That felt good," I thought to myself as I now was standing on my cubicle looking into her eyes.

We both were in sync, but then she glided upward through the roof that didn't exist. I was full of faith through my experiences of low valleys and mountain tops. I flew into the air as I began to experience the dark fog that I previously saw the dancer float through many times. I was able to see everything below us fade, as I broke through this fog. We were spinning in circles now as we continued to spin and grab each other's hands. We twirled for what seemed to be a lifetime. She was in no hurry.

When we stopped, I looked around and saw the cosmos surrounding us and even beyond it. So many galaxies and stars! In the distance I saw a bright kingdom that was very far away. I began to feel one with all of this. My world stopped, and so did time.

Although, time never really seemed to begin in the first place ever since I entered the hallway. It was just like every experience was happening simultaneously as each new thing happened, if that makes any sense.

It was silent.

Now my focus is off the dancer and I turn around in the air to see the milky way. She puts her arms around me and she points to my eyes and then points towards earth. I saw the color turquoise radiating out of my eyes. For a second, I forgot about all my fear, all my anxiety now that I was in this place of eternal bliss.

This place that seemed like outer space, but it was so much more. The best way I could describe it was like the home that I truly belonged in. Acceptance, purpose, individuality, but at the same time a unity with all things.

I had faith in this dancer. I had the ability to zoom in on earth below and see my hometown in Denver, Colorado. Not only could I see my hometown, I could even see my own house with an ambulance outside loading a little boy's body into the truck. With flashing lights, they rushed off to what I assumed to be the hospital.

"What is this?" I asked the dancer, "Is this me? Have I killed myself?"

The dancer stepped close. As what goes up must come down. We gently descended back down through the fog and settled on the concrete.

When my feet hit the ground I saw the giant Door Master running straight at us with a double-edged battle ax! I began to feel very afraid. He was going to chain me up again. He was going to kill me and the dancer!

"I'm dead," I thought to myself, "there's no escaping him."

As the ground shook with every giant step, he ran like a battle warrior. He got closer and closer. The dancer turned with her beautiful turquoise eyes and kissed my forehead. She held her lips on my forehead for what seemed to be a very long time, considering how close the giant was getting to us. As comforting as she was, I was still afraid.

He was now exactly seven feet away. That's too close for kisses. Like a Jedi-tai chi master, she made her move. She crouched down in a Primanti's position. With one hand arched in the air and when the giant was exactly three feet away she turned her body and slowly pushed her opposite hand forward in a fluid, smooth motion.

I saw energy come from her flat hand and hit The Door Master right in the chest without ever touching him. This en-

ergy was effortless and poured out of her with the color of...
yes, you guessed it, turquoise. I'm beginning to like this color a
lot and hope all the people that have been saying that my eyes
have turned turquoise are right. Even though I highly doubt it.
This turquoise energy was amazing. She sent this 8 or 9 foot
giant Door Master, who had no name, flying seventy feet times
seven.

"Woah..." I thought I was afraid of the giant, but any fear I
once had for him was now replaced by a new fear-like respect
for this dancer. She was small but very powerful, more power
than I have ever seen.

Just as fast as he flew back, we danced forward together.
Hand in hand we glided down the hallway of cubicles jumping
through the roof that didn't exist.

Through the fog, I got another glimpse of the cosmos. Again,
time and space stopped for an eternity and then back down we
came, and as I drifted downward through the fog, I saw Greg,
Bernette, and Gabrielle dancing too. Beautifully, they kept up
with us, as we journeyed toward the door that I entered in the
beginning of this very traumatic but enlightening room.

When we were about seven feet away from the door, I saw it
open. Huge turquoise eyes once again engulfed my attention,
shifting me away from everything that was happening. Before
I knew it, I was standing in front of the door facing The Narrator. When I turned to make sure the dancer, Bernette, Greg,
and Gabrielle were all with me, I saw the dancer in her Pri-
mantis positions as she gently sent an energy that pushed me
forward into the arms of The Narrator. Then I heard a SLAM!

The door behind shut. Keeping everyone inside the Trauma Room but me. I screamed for Greg and Gabrielle, but mainly I screamed for my beautiful love, Bernette. I could not leave her alone in that horror room. I banged on the door and turned the glowing knob, but it wouldn't open. The padlock was still there, unlocked, so I didn't understand why it wouldn't open.

I fell to my knees and began to cry when I felt a strong, but gentle arm around my shoulders, pushing down so hard on my right side it caused me to spin around like a ballerina from the Nutcracker. Those huge turquoise eyes glared into my soul once again. This cylinder-like hallway was shining like never before. The precious stones were now turned into diamonds.

I continued to cry and The Narrator brought me to my feet and said, "You have changed Kevin, your eyes are like mine. Walk with me. Not just for the moment but also, what's beyond this moment."

I felt anger and terror pulsing through my body and then I snapped.

Diamond in the Rough:

Chapter 11

I could not believe the audacity The Narrator had to ask me to walk with him after all I've been through.

"Walk with you?" I said to The Narrator, "Wait, wait one second! Do you have any idea what I just went through? Do you have any idea of all the horrible things that go on in this room? Of course, you don't because you weren't there!"

The Narrator responded, "Yes, I told you, though you're stepping into the room alone, I will be with you through all the pain, fear, and anxiety. I told you I have my battles too and most of them are dealing with hurting people in my masterpiece not believing me when I said, 'I am with you.'"

This made me very angry because he was a coward and proved it by not stepping into the room with me. What reason could he possibly have for not coming in? I get it, he may have wanted me to learn a lesson, but that room should never be traveled alone!

My trust is beginning to weaken for The Narrator. This is

all starting to be a bit much. Losing my family without reason or understanding was enough to make me feel crazy. Now the uncertainty of everything I'm going through in these doors is pushing me around like a ping pong ball in an intense two competition with two players. I don't have any room for people coming in and out of my life on their terms. I need answers, I need to know what I'm going to face.

"You were not only gone," I said in a very angry voice, "You were... you were probably hiding! Why didn't you come in with me, if you were not afraid of the room?"

"Just because I didn't step into the room with you, doesn't mean I wasn't around in one way or another, going through everything you experienced, the pain and the beauty."

I replied, "You don't know anything about beauty! I'm alive because of a beautiful dancer in that room not because of you!"

The Narrator then said, "Let me ask, are you hurt physically? You still have to face the Door of Anxiety to prepare you for your purpose. Although, you do have free will. No matter your choice, your path will always lead you here."

"Well... no. I'm not hurt physically, but mentally I'm fried! I saw things you have never dreamed of seeing, if it wasn't for the beautiful dancer I would have never gotten out! You did nothing to help! So leave me alone. I don't trust you or even believe you to be real. I think I'm in a nightmare, nothing more. And I don't want anything to do with you!"

Right then, I noticed the clean-cut businessman Tusk was

close enough to hear our conversation. I wanted to talk to him and I wanted The Narrator gone, as I refuse to go through the other door.

The Narrator had a tear come down his face that sparkled like the diamonds on the wall. In fact, I realized, then, that these diamonds on the walls looked exactly the same as his teardrop.

I thought to myself, "Could all these diamonds on the walls be his tears? Could he have been crying?"

As I stood there in deep thought, he told me, "Kevin, you have free will and have made yourself clear. I still hold to my promises even though you don't believe in me, or this dream of yours to be real. This could be a dream come true for you.

"I want you to know, when you cry, I don't let your tears just fall to waste. I collect them in a Mason jar, and mine too. I have a room filled with Mason jars of all the tears that fall on lonely faces. I make beauty out of tears, as I make beauty out of all types of horrible things in this world.

"Remember the scope I gave you? Each diamond is a teardrop from another person that I sought after. That I chased. I made you a tool that allowed you to see the truth. I leave no waste through the pain. The only thing is, you have to be around long enough to notice it. Do you notice this yet, Kevin?

"See Kevin, this is why I added these diamond tears to this wall. Please, understand, your pain will be avenged. I make beauty out of everything. I made beauty out of my tears and yours together because only you can face your battles, though

I'm with you through your battles, I am facing my battles at this very moment."

Just as he said those words, I felt pressure building up in my body. And I broke down and began to cry once again. I replied in a very broken voice, "Okay…I'll go. Just one more door, right?"

He replied, "I only have one more door for you, whether or not you go through additional doors is up to you. This door is not like the rest, this door will complete my side of the preparation for who you're meant to be.

"I will not go with you. You're stronger than you know and in this room no one, including The Door Master, will be aware of your presence. You will just observe what's beyond the door as long as you want, then you can leave when you want? Fair enough?"

I replied, "Yes, the worst is over I suppose."

So I asked if after this door I can go home to my family.

The Narrator replied, "Now if I told you what you wanted to know you probably wouldn't believe me anyway.One thing about you is that you tend to see the negative in things and hold onto negativity assuming something bad is always around the corner. You will have to remain in this darkness a little while so when you grow into your future. You will understand how bright your future really is! Now I will trust you to go in and out of The Anxiety Room and call my name three times and I will return as fast as I left. I have some projects I will attend to in the meantime."

I turned around and looked for the third door and remembered how fast The Narrator comes and goes, so I turned around to see and just as I suspected he was gone.

I looked at the last and final door and reached for the handle and right before I touched it I head another familiar voice saying "I wouldn't do that if I were you". I turned around and sure enough, it was the businessman, Tusk. I figured this connection I shared with him would come to the surface at some point.

The timing of this encounter is very interesting though, it reminded me of what The Narrator said before…

"Timing is order and the order of time is yet to be determined."

This is very intriguing. Could this be some kind of sign? Could Tusk be some kind of help to me on my quest through The Door of Anxiety?

So I replied, "Oh, hi, Mr. Tusk, why wouldn't you go through this door? Is there something I need to know before I step in?"

Tusk replied in a calmer voice, "Don't be in such a hurry, I've been watching you rush around from one traumatic experience to another. Maybe you should take a break and clear your head for a minute. It might do you some good, don't you think?"

I replied, "Yeah, I suppose. I am tired, and I have been through a lot. Maybe it wouldn't be a bad idea to think this through a bit."

I wasn't sure about this Tusk guy but he did make a valid point in my mind as I have been so worried about getting home I've been willing to go through hell and back many times… at that moment I turned around and faced Tusk and he was right in front of me with his hand out and said, "So… do I get your name now?"

I replied "Yeah, sure… it's Kevin.

"How was The Trauma Room, Kevin?"

I flew off the handle and replied, "'Trauma' doesn't express what I went through! There was a terrifying Door Master who chained me to a bunch of prisoners and The Narrator left me! If it wasn't for the beautiful glowing…"

Tusk interrupted right before I told him about the dancing spirit, "Now, now… Kevin, you don't have to relive all this trauma to explain. I hate seeing you in such pain and misery! I had no idea it was that bad in there. I have never been personally and besides, I understand."

I replied "Really? You never went through these doors? Why not."

He replied, "Well, The Narrator has his way of doing things and I have mine, but we're different. I don't like going through pointless terror from the sounds of it and besides, I'm comfortable where I'm at on my chair. I like my role in all this. I never leave my area. So, yes. I completely understand you, that's why I stay out of it."

"YOU DO?" I asked.

"Yes, Kevin. I understand completely and I love telling you everything you want to hear. It's who I am, I'm a lover of pleasure and it's my pleasure to give you what you love. Now tell me, what do you love?"

Darkness radiated from his eyes, but I felt companionship with Tusk immediately.

I replied, "I feel like there is something off about you, but at the same time I'm hungry for whatever this connection is that we share."

He replied, "I totally agree, Kevin. You may feel like there's something off about me because I'm different and there's nothing wrong with that.

"That Narrator guy, he's a funny one. Always walking around like he owns the place, filling people's heads with nonsense. Retribution and forgiveness, who does he think he is? If he was a remotely good person, why would he put you through such a traumatic experience?

"Really, ask yourself, Kevin, does that make sense? He should put an end to all painful experiences if he was nearly as powerful as he claims to be, don't you think?"

I replied, "Yeah, I have thought about that. Supposedly, there is a prophecy of a warrior that will destroy everything behind these walls."

Tusk replied "Yes, yes, the prophecy. I've heard of this many times and many times different people have come through these doors and never made it out of all three. I see you're coming to the third one and I wanted to talk to you in case I didn't see you again."

I thought to myself, "'Never see me again?' Geez, is that how the prisoners came into place? Does The Narrator bring people in filling their heads with dreams and prophecies? Is he the maker of these rooms trapping people in their worst nightmare by convincing them it's their dream? If so, this Narrator guy is dangerously deceptive. I must hear Tusk out before I make any more rash decisions."

"Do you have a place we could talk, Tusk? I would like to hear what you have to say."

I couldn't help but see that Tusk had an enormous grin on his face. Next, I felt a briskly strong and rough arm around my shoulder, pushing down so hard on the left side of my body he spun me around like a toy doll. Walking at a very fast pace we moved toward his fireplace.

This fireplace was in a huge room with tall ceilings on the other side of the hallway. There were no doors on this side. All three doors were on one side and Tusk had his own area without a door in his living quarters.

There was everything a house would have except it was all in one room. When we got to the fireplace, he had the red leather chair with a very tall back sitting in front of the fire. He had a second identical chair that was sitting across from the first one. Both chairs were around the fireplace, where he had his desk sitting on top of a dark fur rug.

"He must have rearranged everything just for me," I thought

to myself, "How thoughtful."

He took a seat and started twisting his gray mustache, then he said, "Sit, boy sit, I have a great deal for you, a deal you can't refuse."

When I sat down, I noticed he had a piece of paper on my side of the desk next to a very fancy pen made out of pure gold. Next to the pen was a steaming cup of hot chocolate with a handful of marshmallows in it, just how I liked it. He still had that same TV show on, and I started to look closer. The family of rabbits was exactly like mine back home.

I stared at the TV for so long that Tusk said to me, "Do you recognize something about this man?"

"No, it's the rabbits," I replied, "I have one at home that I carved myself and it looks identical. Also, when I was in the room of fear it was one of my memories I kept reliving. See the whole reason I carved this family of rabbits was because I killed them mowing our yard, it was very hard on me. It was like some kind of closure or something… kind of hard to explain."

Tusk replied, "Kevin, what if I told you that you were only in a nightmare right now and me and The Narrator don't really exist. What if I told you that this nightmare is dealing with childhood trauma of your parents getting a divorce? Kevin, they are divorced and you're actually ten years older. You have moved past this divorce and have a family of your own. This man in this show is you. You have a wife named Bernette and two children a five-year-old girl named Rayne and a son that's three, his name is Matthew. You have your own business, working as a successful carpenter.''

My mind started racing. My heart started pounding out of my chest, thinking of being married to Bernette. Everything was starting to make sense now. That's why I loved Bernette so much when I met her! Why didn't I remember our past experiences when I saw her, it's as if we never met. Then again if what he is saying is true, and I am reliving childhood trauma than that would make sense.

Hmm… interesting, I've now been through two out of three rooms and I definitely don't want to see what "The Anxiety Room" has to offer after what I've been through in the first two rooms.

I really don't hate The Narrator, or maybe I do. One thing is for sure though, I can count on him not returning to go through the Anxiety Room with me. I also cannot count on the dancer to be there to help me through it. I have no idea what is behind that door. I have come to the conclusion that Tusk must be right. I must be in a nightmare dealing with childhood trauma. I'm not 100% sure, however, the odds are likely enough to encourage me to move forward with Tusk.Relief came over me as I realized none of this was real.

Next Tusk said, "All you have to do is sign this piece of paper and go through the door at the end of this cylinder hallway. The door labeled, 'Exit from your nightmare plus ten years."

I picked up the pen and almost immediately signed the paper but hesitated.

I remembered thinking to myself what The Narrator said

"timing is order and the order of time is to be determined! Plus ten years is a time frame! Could this be some kind of code? Or maybe a test from The Narrator? Maybe I need to determine the time I'm in. Maybe I'm not a 14-year-old boy. Maybe I'm a grown man and I need to wake up. Me being in a dream makes this whole world make more sense. That would explain how I don't remember getting here and the magical land that has been jerking me around against my free will. All the surprises and terrifying experiences I was able to live through all makes sense with Tusk's alibi.

Tusk than interrupted my thought process and said, "What's the matter, Kevin? Do you not want to wake up to your wife Bernette?"

I said, "Yes, but what does all the fine print say?"

Tusk replied, "Don't sweat the small stuff kid, this paper is only a figment in your imagination, Just as I am. The 'I AM' does not really exist, don't you get it? I don't really exist and neither does The Narrator. You're alone in this nightmare. You're the only one that really exists. Your body has created me as a character in your mind to wake yourself up because you're getting too afraid. It's your bodies way of protecting yourself in your sleep. You have taken all you can take.

"Honestly, there is only you in your real life with your real family. Your wife, and two kids, also, your mom and dad.Nothing you see is real. This is just the only way to tell your brain to wake up, you have to walk through the door I described to you. But first, you must sign the paper. What do you say, Kevin? Do you want to wake up?"

I thought about it for six minutes and came to the conclusion Tusk has confirmed my decision with his reasoning. Now I have no doubts. This is a nightmare and I'm a full grown man. I'm married to Bernette which I why I loved her like I did. It's time to wake up!

I signed the paper.

Next, I stood to my feet and said, "Thank you, Mr. Tusk. Finally, something I want to hear."

Tusk replied, "I will always take pleasure in telling you what you want to hear, so any day kid. I am a man of good news to the ears and sweet taste to the tongue.

"Your signature will relieve you from being allowed on the premise of these hallways which are only a dream. You don't have to worry about any Door Masters or lost souls anymore. You're free to go and I think it's time to get you home."

"Now follow me," he insisted.

We walked back into the hallway that was now filled with diamonds tears, I'm going home to my wife now, I thought to myself. I was very excited. Tusk led me to a door at the opposite end of the cylinder-like hallway that I first entered in the beginning of what I'm now learning to be nothing more than a bad dream. This was a huge dark door with black vines all over the door. These black vines spelled the number six. Also, these black vines spelled out exactly what Tusk told me,

'Exit from your nightmare'
'+10 years.'

"See, everything adds up with this guy," I thought to myself.

Of course, I know there's a very small percentage this Tusk guy could deceive me just as The Door Master in The Fear Room did. I don't like there being this possibility. However, my options are narrowed down to very few possibilities. With the odds being so small I'm being deceived after hearing Tusk's alibi and comparing his alibi to my current options, I'm convinced this is my best course of action. Nonetheless, I except what's behind this door and ready to face the consequences even if I am being deceived. At this point, if there's another Door Master behind this door, I'll just have to figure something out.

Right then, I reached for the doorknob. The knob was made with the face of a lamb and when I touched it, it was very cold. Like a living carcass. It gave me the creeps. But still, I was thinking of one thing and one thing only, my dear Bernette. I gave it a twist and stepped through.

As I stepped through I looked over my shoulder to say good-bye to Tusk who was just behind me, but now all the sudden he was all the way at the other side of the hallway staring at me with his hands rubbing back and forth.

"Bye, Mr. Tusk!" I yelled.

Tusk replied, "See ya later, kid!"

He gave a strange laugh as I closed the door.

There's A Time To Bend:

Chapter 12

My radio is so loud in the mornings. It's obviously better than the traditional alarm clock ringing and piercing my eardrums every morning. So I set the local oldies station to wake me up.

Ugh. Half asleep I rolled over and saw my beautiful wife Bernette.

"THANK GOD I'M HOME! TUSK WAS RIGHT!" I thought to myself.

I loved to watch her sleep so peacefully. It was like the first time I had ever seen her in my bed. In my house that I own. This is so wonderful to be awake. It kind of makes me not want to go back to sleep after that one. I started to get my work jeans on. Then I noticed her starting to move around and she asks me for water in a very tired, groggy type voice. I keep a huge cup of water on my side of the bed.

"Here you go, baby," I said.

She chugged almost all my water, as usual. I took the cup back to refill it and one of my dreads fell in the cup.

"Gross," I thought to myself and put the cup down.

I keep my dreads neat and clean. They're the thin type of dreads, not the unkempt thick blunt dreads most people think of, even though I like that style on some people. I've been growing my dreads since I was a kid, and they're about down to my waist now. My dreads are very blonde with a few turquoise dreads and a few purple dreads. I grabbed my hair tie and put my dreads up for work. By this time my wife rolled over and asked me about my schedule for the day.

I said, "Oh, I only have a few bids and then I'll be home. I may go to the hookah lounge and write a bit but I'll let you know for sure after my bids."

"Okay. That's fine, babe."

Next, I said in an unusual manner, "Hey babe, so last night I had the craziest dream. I was in this hallway and went through this room and you were there telling me about the house fire. We were all in chains and it felt so real!!"

She responded, "Kevin you have had this dream before and we've talked about this. It's just a dream. It's just childhood trauma, that's all. The divorce was really hard on you baby you almost died as a kid."

I responded "Don't say that! I did not try to kill myself."

Bernette softly responded, "Sweetheart, if you don't accept

what you did, you will never heal and you will keep having night terrors. You got to seek help."

I kinda was mad but her beautiful face calmed me down.

Confused I started thinking to myself and said, "Okay. Well, I'm going to head to the coffee shop. I love you" as I kissed her goodbye.

I walked out the door and she said yelled back, "I love you, baby!"

My mornings are so special to me. Getting my coffee and having the freedom to start my work when I feel like it. A hot latte with one pump of vanilla is the way I like it. Not too sweet. I just like the vanilla taste in my latte. I stopped drooling over my "imaginary" coffee and stepped into my Chevy Avalanche.

It's a pretty sweet Avalanche. It's the all metal Avalanche, not the kind with plastic running halfway up the sides. It has leather, heated and cooled seats, and a sunroof, just like I always wanted.

Life was pretty good. My truck just got back from the Regency factory. They blacked out the taillights, and windows, that's all the Regency package actually does.

I pull through the coffee shop drive-thru in a hurry, because I had an estimate with a guy named Chris at 9:30 and needed to hurry to get there on time. I arrived 9 minutes early and wrote out the basic information for the contract on the job. The job that I was confident I was going to get.

I always said, "If I can get the estimate, I can get the job."

When the time came, I walked up the narrow walkway to the door and gave it three soft knocks, I never want to come on too strong. My dreads are the first thing my customers see, also the first obstacle I have to overcome. Once they see me sell my knowledge to them and I show them my profile. I have fifty-four reviews maintaining a 4.8-star average. I show them pictures of previous jobs, that's usually enough to get respect for my career history. After a few seconds, I saw a strait-laced looking man staring at me.

"Hi," I said in a salesman like voice.

He responded, "Hi, are you 'Kevin'?"

"I am," I responded.

"Come in, come in," he said in a nice voice.

We walked around the job and I wrote it up for $2,200. I decided I would build some more rapport with Chris before I delivered the numbers to him. He asked me about my personal life, which I thought was a little strange.

I asked, "So... Chris what do you do for a living?"

He responded, "Well I'm the youth pastor for Bread of Life Nondenominational Church, at the top of the hills in God's country."

"Wow," I thought.

I don't usually get impressed when people are religious. I believe religion is the cause for most, if not all, spiritual confusion, especially when it comes to Christianity. I thought now is as good as any other time to deliver the numbers to him. When I gave him my pitch, he quickly declined and low balled me at $1,500. My price was $500 below fair market value. I knew this was not a man I wanted to work for. On my way out I tripped over a little boy.

"I'm so sorry," I said after I helped the cute boy up.

He looked oddly familiar.

Chris said, "That's my son, Greg".

"Greg," I thought?

Strange. Something is off about this.

"Today is my birthday, my Dad is taking me to Legoland today than were having boys night at a hotel!"

"He's turning seven tonight," Chris said with a smile, "Yep, no girls allowed. Just a father-son kind of thing for 'the big seven B-day party'."

"Well, that's good," I said, "Happy birthday Greg, it was very nice to meet you!"

"You too, Mister Artist Man," Greg said in a cute voice, as I shut the door behind me.

As soon as I got into my truck, I started thinking about my

dream the night before and remembered Greg in his cubicle.

"It couldn't be." I thought to myself, "That wasn't real!" A flood of memories of the night before began to terrify me.

I shut my brain off as I convinced myself I was putting connections where they don't belong. "Must be a coincidence." I thought to myself. After my first estimate, I had one more estimate to go to. I wasn't sure what her name was, I forgot to ask over the phone. After my customer opened the door, her eyes sparked when she saw me.

"You must be Kevin!"

"I am," I responded.

"Come on in, let me show you around."

She was so sweet. After I went through my selling routine, she hired me on the spot. We talked for an hour and a half after she hired me. She started telling me about a weight loss surgery she would be having that evening and how she was nervous. She said they had to implant a metal device in her stomach for six months. she has gotten counsel and thought about this for years and she's ready to make the decision.

"I'm ready," she said excitedly.

I thought it was strange. I had some red flags going off up in my brain...I'm just going insane. It's probably me. SHUT UP BRAIN! I'm beginning to feel a little crazy after all these memories are merging together with repeated lines and characters.

"It must be a coincidence," I thought to myself.

We wrapped up our conversation, I was walking out and I asked her, "Oh Hey I forgot to get your name."

"Gabrielle," she replied.

I felt my face go pale in an instant.

She asked, "Are you okay, Kevin?"

I responded, "Yes, I'm good. I'll see you in the morning. Have a good day."

I started stumbling to my truck as my world was spinning. As I shuffled my way into my front seat, I reach for my prescribed Xanax bottle and quickly took 2 mg to calm myself before I suffocated. I felt like the walls were closing in.

"This cannot be happening right now. This cannot be happening right now." I thought to myself, "What are the odds. I mean I just had this crazy long, elaborate dream last night and when I wake up, my two bids are the two lost souls that were in chains and my wife is the third lost soul I met!

"THIS CAN'T BE A COINCIDENCE! I mean if this is real, this seven-year-old boy is about to be raped by his youth pastor father tonight. I refuse to let this happen. Gabrielle is about to ruin her quality of life by having this surgery. I have to do something. I have to stop this! How can I stop this?

Okay, I will go home and talk to my wife and let her know what's going on, and then I'll wait at Legoland and find Greg's dad Chris and tell him I know of his plans and put the fear of God in him. As far as Gabrielle is concerned, I'll have to call her and come up with something brilliant to change her mind. Ahh…"

This is my brilliant plan as my Xanax started to hit.

I began calming myself and headed home. When I walked in the front door of my house, my wife had already set the dinner table.

She's so amazing. Such a servant, we only knew each other for a month before we got married. She was from a Mennonite family when I met her and I heard from mutual contacts of how she was in a house fire when she was twelve. I met her when I was twenty-one and she was twenty-three. I admired her outlook on life and spiritual life after such a horrific story of losing her sisters and her mom in the fire. If anyone had an excuse to be mad at the world it was her, yet she was happy. I knew I wanted to marry her right away because of this fact alone.

She greeted me, "How was your day, babe?"

"It wasn't good," I said, "Remember my dream that you say is recurring? I think I'm still in it."

She laughed and said, "Um, babe that's not okay. Like, that's kinda mentally unstable, don't you think?"

I continued, "I know how this sounds, but you don't understand, I actually met the lost souls today."

"What?!?"

"I mean Greg and Gabrielle! Greg is turning seven tonight and in my dream, that's the night his dad rapes him. Babe, his dad is a youth pastor and I made a phone call and got a hold of the senior pastor and found out there have been a few instances in the church that the senior pastor feels uncomfortable with, but there's nothing substantial yet. I think it's real, baby, I need you to trust me."

"I mean so what are you saying, I'm not real?"

"Well, that's what's confusing. You were in my dream too, and you told me about the fire, but that obviously already happened when you were twelve. Check this out though, Gabrielle was my second estimate and she too is having her surgery tonight. It's a stomach surgery, where they implant a metal device in her stomach. According to my dream, the device gets lodged in a main artery and she becomes a ticking time bomb."

"Woah, that is a little strange. This is kind of giving me anxiety, Kevin. Because where does that leave me, I mean, am I just a figment of your imagination?"

"I mean... I'm not sure yet. I'm still figuring all this out, babe. If it makes you feel better does this feel real? Like, does me and you feel real?"

"Yes," my wife responded.

"A wise man once told me that perception is what makes what we think to be real... well, real. Let's use that to our advantage and assume me and you are real. Regardless, I know we're real. If I am in a dream I know when I grow up we will meet and live this life we have and much more. We are soulmates I believe that more than anything."

"Okay, so what are you going to do then?"

"I have to try and stop this from happening," I replied.

"Babe," she exclaimed, "You can't just go kidnap a seven-year-old and tell the cops you had a dream that his pastor dad was going to rape him!"

"That's not my plan, Bernette! Just trust me while I figure this out."

Then my wife said with a smile, "I trust you".

No Solutions:

Chapter 14

In this chapter, I will come to no solutions. As Chapter 13 does not exist, Chapter 14 will explain nothing. This chapter will make no sense. This chapter will serve you no purpose. Or perhaps that is the purpose of this chapter. As the number fourteen never gives you any solutions to the problem.

I will keep this short and sweet. I'm scared. My wife thinks I'm a bit wacky. I don't know what's real and what's not real. All I know is I must keep moving forward and I must save these people from my dream.

I didn't tell my wife about everything in my dream. I left out all the details. She seems to think she knows the dream, as I supposedly have had this dream over and over. But this time it's different. This time I know I made a mistake by making that deal with Tusk. That's what she doesn't know. That slimy guy... he got me on my innocence. I really met Greg, I really met Gabrielle, on the same day the very tragedy that brought us together in the first place... in that horrible Trauma Room. This is proof to my consciousness that I actually am still a boy in a dream or a near death experience that I can't escape from.

None of this is real. Except Greg, Gabrielle, and my wife. In reality, wherever I'm at as a boy, my wife is still a child and so am I. I think when I wake up, we will find each other when we become adults. I'll never know for sure until I can get out of this stupid dream or whatever this is. I signed that stupid contract without reading the fine print. I know how contracts work, with operating a construction business, the fine print will get you. I bet he's got me stuck here for good. I'm probably in a coma back in Denver or something.

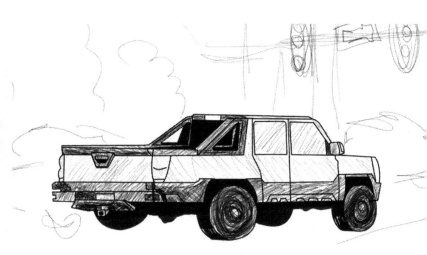

Search and Rescue:
Chapter 15

I decided I would drive up to Legoland and wait. I waited and waited but I saw no sign of Greg or his dad. I went and got some food and ate in a hurry to returned to my stake out spot when I saw Chris, walking around in the Legoland store with his son. I thought about how I was going to go about doing this. I got nothing, so I just walked in.

I went straight up to Chris and said, "Hey Chris..."

He responded, "Kevin? What are you doing here?"

I said, "I need to talk to you Chris... alone."

Chris continued, "Alone? About what? Are you following us?"

I said, "No, not yet. Why don't you tell your son to look around before I drag you out of this store. You won't get away with this."

Chris speaks facetiously now, "Ugh... to think, I almost hired a lunatic. Get away before I call the cops for harassment."

He had his hand out like he was shooing me off and I smacked it away, and then I got in his face and said, "Listen, pal. You may be a youth pastor but I want you to know, I know! I know your plans with the boy tonight and I won't let it happen."

Next thing I know, mall security showed up. Chris, of course, made me look crazy and I was escorted out. So, I called the police and tipped them off with his phone number. I knew I couldn't stop it from happening. Not without proof. This was really eating at me.

I drove around and dialed Gabrielle's number from my Bluetooth headset.

"Hello," She answered.

I responded, "Ughh... Hey, listen to me. I know this sounds crazy, but you can't have this surgery today. Don't go through with it!" I begged.

She said, "Um, what? Thanks for the concern, Kevin. But it's none of your business with all due respect."

I said bluntly, "But it is. We have met in another life. I had a dream about you in a room and you told me about this surgery, the device will get lodged in your main artery and they won't be able to get it out without killing you.

"Hello...?"

"Hello...?"

"Kevin, you're fired." She said coldly.

Click.

I let out a loud scream and broke my phone.

This is hopeless. I'm locked in this nightmare, when now I realize, I was right where I was supposed to be. I should have gone through the last door in that beautiful hallway and everything would have worked out. I should have trusted The Narrator.

Tusk deceived me and stole my dream. I should have overcome all those adversities while I had the chance. Now I can't save anyone. I got to a place where depression took me over again. I was ready to end it all. I wasn't sure if it would work but it was worth trying. My reality was a lie, my children were a lie, and my wife was a lie. How could I live my life knowing that I'm stuck in a coma somewhere? How can I go on knowing I'm not the man I'm meant to be?

I decided to stop by the pawn shop and pick up a .38 revolver. I thought about leaving my wife a note, but what's the point when I know her existence will end with me when I perish. I know she's only a figment of my imagination.

After I picked out the revolver of my choice I drove deep out into the mountains. There were a lot of trees around. I was covered in shade. Beautiful plants were all around. So much life. So much beauty reminded me of the glowing dancer.

I pulled my truck under a huge pine tree. I put it in park and put on my favorite song, "Fast Car" by Tracy Chapman. After listening to the song I stepped out on the grass and fell on my face. I was terrified this wouldn't work. How could I take my life when I'm dreaming. What if I only make this worse? What if I don't die but I live in a coma in this timeline or realm as well? I took the six-shooter and decided to put three bullets in it. Give life a chance right? I raised the snub nose to my head and right before I pulled the trigger, it clicked!

Not the gun!

The truth of all this. Everything in this story makes sense to me now. Three bullets, three doors, three feet, three...

The Narrator had said, "If you ever get to the end of your rope and you can't go any further, call my name three times and I'll be there instantaneously!"

I began to feel excited to see The Narrator. I knew he would come.

I stood to my feet and prepared myself fast. I couldn't think of what I would say to him but only what he would say to me. So I screamed at the top of my lungs "NARRATOR!!! NARRATOR!!! NARRATOR!!!"

I felt a great earthquake that lasted for 7 seconds. I was on my knees, terrified at this great earthquake. When it was over

I lifted my head, and not only was The Narrator staring at me but so was the beautiful dancer. They both stood there, silent, shoulder to shoulder. They both watched me with their turquoise eyes. Those comforting eyes.

The Narrator broke the silence and said, "Well done, Kevin. You have made it through a lot and you're at the end of yourself. You have surrendered. You called on me and I'm here, as I always have been. So has my close companion, the Mime. We never left you, we only let you use your free will.

"However, we always knew you would come back. Like I said you have a mission, Kevin. You have battles to fight in this moment and beyond. Lost Souls tormented by various Door Masters need to be saved. This is your dream; your dream that's dying to become a reality. This is who you're meant to be.

"I'm sorry you have been deceived by Tusk. He and I have a detailed history, a history that started in the beginning of my artwork. He was my friend, apart of another beautiful but separate painting I made a long time ago. This painting had a purpose of its own.

"Tusk was created in my painting along with a lot of other beautiful creatures but none like Tusk. He was the most beautiful and most powerful entity in all of my paintings. When he learned of the fullness of my plans to create my masterpiece. He knew of this very painting of a canvas. This canvas that was me. This masterpiece that was you. I knew he grew jealous and prideful for not being a part of my masterpiece painting and he left our friendship in ashes. He hated me and deep down he hates you and everyone like you because I have created you like me in this canvas of a painting.

Tusk's response.... It hurt me, even though I knew it would happen before I ever created his separate painting long ago. I still loved him regardless of the darkness he would bring into the world. He used his will to force a place into my masterpiece painting by creating a new energy. This energy darkened his name. He became Tusk, 'The Door Master of Deception.'

"The Hallway of Tears is mine. No one can destroy that sacred place. Tusk has a door and you walked through this door to come to this timeline. The is The Door Master of all Door Masters and he wanted to bring you here. He did this because if you die in this timeline you will die in real life. This timeline is every bit a real as any other timeline. However, you don't have all the life experiences of growing up through your teenage years to deal with the confusion that comes along with jumping timelines. You must be patient.

"So I ask you to walk with me once more, not just for the moment but also what's beyond the moment. Kevin, you have gone through so much and I have never left you. This is my masterpiece painting and that includes this timeline ten years after you wake up.

"Everything you have been looking for is right in front of you. Your wife is real. I mean, in a way. You are still a child in reality and so is she. You will have to grow into this timeline. But first, you have to protect all the lost souls from the trauma not in this timeline but behind the doors, where the bondage is all rooted. Set the prisoners free and you will grow to find freedom manifest itself into reality, in your life and the life of all the lost souls, that is the lost souls that are willing. Only you can face your battles. Now I ask you, are you willing to face them?"

"Yes," I replied.

"Now, you no longer need our guidance in person to show you the way. We are the way. Together, you included with us. You surrender to us includes you in what we do. You're ready to become one with the Mime and I.

"This was always my plan to include you, but your trust and belief in our union is what makes it all possible to begin with because of your free will. As it is written on my canvas. This canvas is me, this canvas is you. The brushstrokes of paint are now dried, and I will finish my masterpiece through you, and others after you, but never forget it's because of me and because of you choosing to be one with me."

Then, with both of their turquoise eyes staring into mine, The Narrator and The Mime spoke simultaneously in a loud thunderous voice and said, "I EXIST! I EXIST! I EXIST!"

Just as instantaneously as they showed up together, a great FORCE smashed both The Narrator and The Mime into each other creating a loud "Bang!" The glowing light and turquoise colors swirled around each other for three minutes making all kinds of geometric patterns.

After the time was up and the colors settled I saw something amazing. Instantly, I believed my eyes were turquoise. Instantly, I believed I would carry their spirit with me after I put on this gift that was left behind.

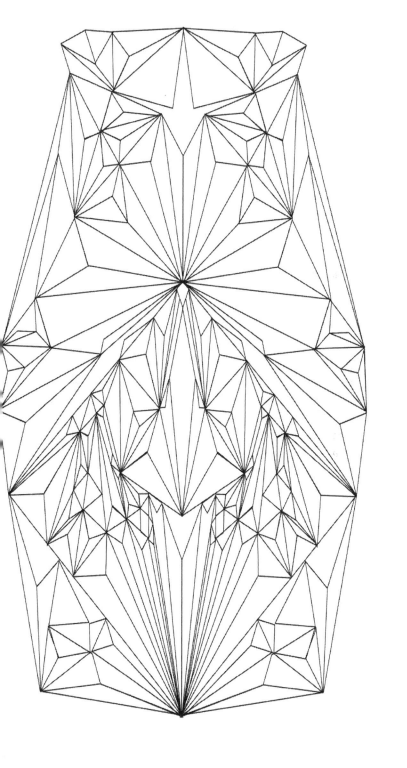

The Ceremony:

Chapter 16

Now that I had turquoise eyes. I saw everything different. The lost souls, Tusk, The Narrator, and the Mime. Even my real life as a boy and my family. Everything had changed now that I believed my eyes had changed. I had seen the truth; I was indeed in a near death experience, my cubicle was true, the paintings were real. I believed I was really a boy.

Now that I know Tusk is evil I remember that he was the one who told me I was an adult married to Bernette, he twisted the truth and brought me to a different timeline through witch-craft, hoping to kill me because he knew how confused I would be. I mean, I almost killed myself with a gun. Timing is order and I have to live my real life before it was too late… It wasn't until I went out of Tusk's door that I believed I was a grown man. What a deceiver he is. Now that I'm here, I'm not afraid of what I have to do. All of my fears were imaginary. Fear only exists in the mind that creates its presence.

As I glared ahead, I heard a voice ask me, "Kevin, what do you see?"

I answered, "I see armor hovering at eye level."

Then I heard the voice say, "What else do you see?"

I replied, "I see a helmet."

This helmet was sharp looking. It was a full-face helmet that had a long nose piece. It had an eye engraved at the center of the forehead, which represented the holding place of my DMT. That was just another indication I was having a DMT experience. My eyes told me this helmet, represented that I have been claimed. My soul has been claimed by The Narrator.

Next, I saw a metal breastplate covered in spastic designs with turquoise colors radiating out of each design. My eyes told me this breastplate, represented my actions, and that my actions had now been made right, by the sacrifice of The Narrator and The Mime.

Then, I saw a double-edged longsword, with a handle that had the face of a lamb. The lamb was radiating this beautifully, now infamous, turquoise color energy. It was piercing out of the lamb's eyes. The sword had an ancient text, in an ancient language, engraved on the side of the blade. This sword represented the spirit that now existed within me, the beautiful dancer and The Narrator alike.

Then there was a belt. This belt was thick, made out of tree root. It too had designs, and ancient text covering this belt, representing the truth of all life, all the living organisms and things we cannot perceive through our senses.

I saw a magnificent shield. This shield was tall enough to

cover all the way from my shoulders to my ankles. It had a long flat rectangular shape. My eyes told me this shield, represented my faith, that I was right where I needed to be, and every action from now on served a purpose in the bigger picture, in the overall painting.

Lastly, I saw boots that glowed pure white. They looked light as a feather, just like my dad always said. These shoes represented the fact that this armor is available to everyone. Peace was available to all who wore these.

Then, the voice said, "Kevin, you have seen correctly. Now go. Kevin, do what needs to be done."

Just like that, the voice was gone. I knew what needed to be done. I strapped into my armor fiercely and sheathed my sword along my left side, because I am right-handed. I was filled with love, joy, peace, patience, kindness, goodness, gentleness, faithfulness, and self-control. I was also filled with purpose. A purpose to end the doors in my life, and also all the souls that lived within the doors. It was my responsibility to lead a great battle. A battle to remember.

I was ready for battle. I was ready to save the lost souls from my dreams, my dreams to make them free. I was ready to destroy anything that got in my way. Now the only problem was I had to decide how I wanted to get back to the cylinder hallway that led me to the doors in the first place as The Narrator didn't give me any clear instructions.

That funny guy, it's like he gives you exactly what you need to be protected from yourself, but he refuses to baby you. He's a huge believer in overcoming adversity. It's like when you don't learn a lesson he will allow you to relive certain things to make sure you get it right. To make sure you learn. Why? This reason right here is why. I'm standing here and this time I will not fail, this time I will not be afraid, this time I won't let adversity keep me from moving forward.

I walked around waiting for a sign. Even though I couldn't find anything right away, I knew The Narrator was with me and I "imagined" the dancer twirling in front of me. I paced around the mountains and started to climb. When I couldn't find a sign, I decided to look up. The mountain was beautiful. I had no water, and no food, but still I climbed knowing if I fell to my death it would really kill me one way or another. With my shield strapped to my back, I moved like a lion, ready to pounce on its prey.

I had climbed for hours when I finally saw a cave. The cave was dark, it was moistened and dirty. Normally, this cave would make me afraid. I felt no fear. Only amazing love, this amazing love that destroys fear on contact. So I marched forward into the darkness of this unknown cave. When I stepped in, my eyes radiated light everywhere I went, and all the spiders crawled back into the cracks in which they came from. A slave amongst slaves, and gods amongst gods. They hid from the light protruding from my eyes. This cave was like a maze with moving walls. I was willing to make myself lost, so I could be found.

After a while of being lost, I saw the portal I needed, the portal to the other side. This was a drop-off. A certain death this cliff was, but with my shield of faith, it was whatever I decided it to be. When I directed my eyes downward, I could see for miles. Right as I took seven steps back, I took seven strides forward. I had no fear. My eyes closed softly and I let my body lay flat in the air, with nothing below for miles. I descended into the beyond.

I fell for miles. I went into the deep subconscious of the earth and the heavens. I landed suddenly, with my fist in the ground to disperse the energy from my fall, making a hole in the concrete several inches down. I had landed kneeling with my helmet facing the rock below. I slowly lifted my head to glare at the back of the door that once deceived me. The door that belongs to The Door Master of all Door Masters. Tusk….

On the back of this door, I saw the name "Jazmine" in my mother's handwriting. I knew there was no way through but to break the door down. I love my mother and I began to fall into a witch type trance idolizing my mother's handwriting.

Right then I heard a loud voice, like a human voice and it said, "1,2,3, CLEAR!"

I had blurry vision, human vision again and I could see my 14-year-old arm bandaged up and doctors all around me. When I looked at the screen monitoring my heart, I saw the zig-zag lines go flat. I saw my limp body and looked around the room. The doctors were recharging and about to hit me again.

You know how time doesn't exist on the other side? I gently laid flat on top of what was my soon to be corpse, and zap! I was back in my armor staring at the door with my mom's name.

"I see," I thought to myself, "This is it. Every move I make must be methodical, as timing is order, but wisdom also is in order." This door is nothing more than another slimy trick from Tusk.

As I marched forward, I put my shield of faith in front of my body. I stood in front of my mother's name on this door Tusk made. I was mesmerized by the thought of her. Again a deceiver this man Tusk is, and as a deceiver, he should have the death of a deceiver. The kind he deserves. I gave my mom's name one last look. I then threw my shoulder forward with one smooth stroke and the door shattered into pieces.

Annihilation:

Chapter 17

I strapped my shield to my back, as Tusk frantically ran up to me and accused me saying, "Young boy, you signed my contract and I own you. You have no power here, these souls belong to me, and you are in another timeline".

I turned and looked at him. I glared at him right in the eyes and I saw nothing but darkness.

"Tusk, I'm an artist of a masterpiece canvas, this canvas is not you. Your powers only apply to those who do not possess the turquoise eyes."

Right then he noticed the color of my eyes and fell to the ground. I continued to step forward towards Tusk and he continued to crawl backwards with a terrified look on his face.

I said, "You were made to be destroyed. But since I'm an artist, I save the best for last."

I got into position, with one hand arched in the air just like I saw The Mime do before me, and I harvested the power of truth from my belt and swiftly pushed my other hand forward. My hand was strong and flat and the truth of my words came radiating through my hand and sent Tusk flying so fast, he slammed into his red chair and the chair flew back to his fireplace. Tusk fell to the ground shaking in fear. His dark rug started to catch on fire.

I turned around and marched on to a door, The Trauma Room. The padlock was still unlocked and the torch was still hanging on the right side of the door. I grabbed the torch and walked through the door, I was ready for battle. I was ready for my purpose and to create the kind of ending I wanted to see for myself despite all the pain I had to go through to get to where I am.

I was so afraid the last time I was in this room. Things seem to be so different now that I know the truth and what's actually going on. I didn't learn this information by someone telling me, I learned this information by going through the motions of passion and torment, also going through the knowledge of not knowing and proceeding even when I felt like giving up. This was a perfect storm of events to create a great warrior with untapped potential. I was ready to see what I could do, so I began screaming.

"Door Master!!! Come face me!!!"

The glow from my armor lit the entire room, all the way up through the roof that didn't exist and into the cosmos, which gave me the idea of my next plan of action. I had to see the cosmos one last time before this room was destroyed. As I was thinking this, I heard the giant running fast.

I unwrapped my shield and jumped through the roof that didn't exist and through the fog. I got one last look at the beautiful cosmos and once again time stood still. As what goes up must come down, this time I came down with a sword. With my elbows lifted high, and both hands on my sword handle, I began, not only to come down, but I began to pick up momentum. I saw The Door Master looking for me, then he looked up...

As precisely as I strike wooden blunt objects, the tip of my blade came down, hard, in the middle of forehead piercing his body, all the way down into the cold concrete floor. As I jerked my sword back toward my chest, his body split in two pieces.

His blood ran down to my feet. Then, I began to take his blood and mark the foreheads of everyone in the room that was to die. I walked down the long aisle of screaming prisoners. One by one, I marked their heads and set them on fire. I came to the firefighters that tried to save Bernette's sisters and breathed the breath of life into their forehead, and their shackles broke free.

Afraid, they stared at me and I said, "Do not be afraid, you are a part of a great battle."

They believed me and made torches out of the burning bodies and wood. I told them to take the blood of The Door Master and mark the forehead of every dead thing. They listened, and as they marked the foreheads, I burned the bodies. Greg and Gabrielle came at that moment, already in belief, they knew exactly what to do. They began marking foreheads.

We burned so much in this room, but we saved more than we burned. Still, there was another soul I needed to find: my soulmate. The soulmate I would find when I awaken from this dream of mine to destroy these doors and set the living free. I could not find Bernette, but I knew where to go. I went to her old cubicle, where she was previously chained to. I saw her crying, staring at her paintings of her sisters.

I told her, "You have to make a choice Bernette. Let go or be let go of."

She looked into my eyes and kissed my cheek. Next thing I knew, she had my torch in her hand and burned all her painful memories, she made into painful paintings.

Then, she turned around and said, "I wasn't crying because I was holding on, I was crying because I was saying goodbye."

"Very good, let's move."

As we traveled through this dark room with screaming voices and burning flesh, I told my small group "We must move quickly."

Then when we got to the door I screamed, "WE MUST BURN THE BODY OF THE DOOR MASTER!"

We all took a turn in setting a body part on fire until he was engulfed by flames.

I opened the door and they all stepped into the sacred hallway built by the maker, The Narrator. I gave The Trauma Room one last look and I told Greg to throw the torch into it and slammed the door shut!

"Now the padlock," I thought to myself, "No one's getting out!"

I asked Gabrielle to snap the padlock shut like the cuffs were snapped shut on all the prisoners.

Fear's Last Breath:
Chapter 18

I looked at the few freed souls that I had as a small army, and I told them, "Soon, we will grow. The Door of Fear will not be the same as The Trauma Room. The Door Master will not look scary like your's did. She will be deceiving and take an innocent form. However, all the prisoners will be bound by chains, but not in cubicles. It will be a crowd of people in formal lines. Row by row, every prisoner will be in a paralyzing trance by the beauty of The Door Master.

"I will go in first and kill The Door Master. When you hear the release cry out of all the prisoners, that's when you will enter. When she dies, the trance will be broken and everyone will realize what has been done to them. They will deal with the trauma of being in a fear-like state of mind for an eternity.

"They will look innocent, but don't be fooled. Evil exists within every door. I will send a turquoise light radiating out of my eyes and everything that lives will also have glowing eyes. Every eye that does not glow, you will mark their foreheads with The Door Master's blood, and we will burn everyone without eyes to see."

They all stared at me. We march 7 steps to the door and I said, "Wait for The Door Master's cry, and do your work."

As I looked at The Door of Fear, I didn't wait to admire the work that went into making the sign, I just kicked the door right off the hinges and told my followers, "We won't need a padlock for this door."

I stepped in alone and saw an altar with a throne on it, The Throne of Fear. On this throne sat a woman with enticing beauty, to the eyes, but death to the soul.

She looked at me and immediately grabbed her two daggers. She ran towards me. I threw the faceguard of my helmet down towards my chin and I ran to meet her death.

As I got closer, her beautiful face quickly changed to a monstrous appearance that would be terrifying to someone without my shield, which was now in front of my body. As she struck at my head with her dagger, I lifted my shield. The two metals clashed together, and as I pushed forward with my shoulder, she began to fall to the floor. I stabbed my sword through her shin so she couldn't move. Then I stood over her face, which was now turned to beauty again.

I knew she was seductive, but I had seen her true colors, even before she ever showed them to me. I lifted my shield in the air and struck her neck with the bottom blunt side of this shield. Her head and shoulders were separated by a puddle of blood. I struck so hard that I had to pull my shield out from the concrete with all my might. At that moment, a horrible screech filled the room.

My followers came in and handed me the torch. Taking the blood of this door master, they began to mark all the foreheads of the living dead. All the souls with glowing eyes were set free. After every forehead was marked, I looked behind me and my army had grown three times bigger.

I looked into all of the living's eyes and shouted, "We stand for truth!"

My army shouted back, "ONE TRUTH!"

With the torch in my hand, I said, "We stand for faith!"

My army shouted back, "ONE FAITH!"

With my sword in the air, I said, "We stand for love!"

My army shouted back, "ONE LOVE!"

Then I turned and dropped the torch on the crowd of the living dead. They all burned as the room began to smell. I dropped the torch in front of my army.

I yelled, "WE MARCH!"

My army had my respect as we left The Fear Room. I told them, "If you want to see the death of The Door Master guarding The Door of Anxiety, who has tortured me personally in my life, I welcome you to witness me kill this master, this master of anxious torture. This is personal. If you're with me…"

"I say 'Annihilation' and you will reply, 'One Love.'"

I shouted "ANNIHILATION!"

Like a roaring lion, I heard my army respond, "ONE LOVE!!!"

I shouted "ANNIHILATION!"

They responded again, "ONE LOVE!"

"You may all witness this great death of an evil entity. This time, the padlock is needed. Bernette, please hand me the torch."

Bernette grabs the torch, and while she hands it to me, she whispers "I believe in freedom."

I replied, "I believe in chains... chains that need to be broken."

I paced back and forth, getting my army ready for battle and I began to yell in passion,

I shouted in passion "ANXIETY HAS NO PLACE IN HUMANITY!"

My army replied, "ONE LOVE! NO FEAR!"

I continued, "Anxiety has plagued humanity and this room is filled with a great population, all of which are innocent. NO FOREHEAD WILL BE MARKED IN THIS ROOM EXCEPT THE FOREHEAD OF THE DOOR MASTER HIMSELF, AND THE DOOR MASTER IS MINE TO KILL."

My army replied, "ONE LOVE! NO FEAR!"

I then asked my final question, "ARE... YOU... WITH TRUTH?!?!"

My army responded, "ONE TRUTH! NO FEAR! NO TRAUMA! NO ANXIETY!"

It seemed we were all in one accord. I turned around and opened the door, and with my army behind me, we marched. Nothing was around yet. All the people were up on risers. Thousands of people up in the air looking down at us. I walked into the middle of the room, and my army made a wide circle around me. I waited... I waited.

Then I yelled out, "Door Master!!! Come face your prey, who is no longer your prey!!!"

Nothing happened. When I looked down I was standing on wood. This was odd, everything around was concrete. I got on my knees and ripped the wood off its holding place and there stood a child with black eyes.

This child had sharp teeth, yet looked terrified. This was no child. This one only takes the form of a child, because of how weak anxiety really is.

I grabbed the child and held him in the air. The child began screeching and clawing for my neck. What goes up must come down. I brought this evil entity's body down on my knee with such force I broke his back in half. I then dropped his body on the floor. As the child wiggled around, repeating an ancient language in a very deep voice. The child refused to look at me while it was attempting to crawl in the opposite direction. I grabbed the entity's ankle and dragged it towards myself and put my foot on his chest, my foot that was fitted with the armor of peace. I took my sword of the spirit, the spirit of The Narrator, The Mime, myself, and now also the spirit of this great army. Everyone in the room watched as I cut The Door Master's wrist in a horizontal motion.

I took its blood with my fingertips and marked his forehead. He cried for mercy but I gave him none. I was going to kill this door master. I had a personal vendetta with anxiety but then I realized I wasn't the only one. As the leader, I let all the living down off the risers and I handed the torch to my new army that grew in great numbers and said, "Burn him. Burn everything!"

When finally the room had turned to ash, my army was now thousands. They filled the hallway shoulder to shoulder. After I locked the padlock of the last burning room, I made my way through my crowd of followers to find Tusk. I followed the flames. I followed his fear. I saw him sitting in his red leather chair laughing.

He said, "You think you won, you can't kill me. I'm an entity, I will leave this body and go to the next."

I replied, "I know, but you're old and washed out. I expect a good fight next time we meet. I think it's time you found a new body."

Then I grabbed him by the throat I noticed him twisting his mustache, laughing. I lifted him in the air. I took my sword and pressed it firmly below his chin and with an upward stroke his mustache quickly turned red. My blade came out of the top of his head.

I screamed, "THIS WAS NOT PLANNED!!! THIS WAS NOT A CRY FOR ATTENTION!!!"

This battle was finished. I turned around with what was left of Tusk's body in my hand.

I said to my army, "Follow me!"

We passed through the hole in the wall that used to hold the deceptive door which used to read 'Exit from your nightmare, plus 10 years.'"

Now that I had destroyed it with my shield, there was wood everywhere.

I gripped Tusk's neck because I refused to lose his body. His body must too burn, but I will not disrespect the hallway of The Narrator's diamond tears.

Since Tusk had no door except this one, I thought it would be the perfect place to watch him burn. As soon as my whole army made it through the door, we were inside of the mountain cave in which I came. We all grabbed a piece of wood and I looked at his body. So frail, so weak now, as I stared into the darkness of his eyes.

I set the first piece of wood on Tusk's mouth. Out of the heart the mouth speaks and I speak death over this entity, Tusk.

After me, every person in my army played a role in burning

Tusk. He had orchestrated of all these horrific rooms. The smell of his burning flesh moved our feet out of the mountains rather fast. We walked out through the caves through which I had come, and back from the mountain top. My whole army journeyed down this mountain, and as we were making our way down, I was stretching my leg down towards the nearest rock in mid-stride, when I heard a loud overpowering voice.

"1, 2, 3, CLEAR!"

Again I was back as a little boy, looking at all the doctors. I could see my mom in the hallway looking through the glass, then I noticed the screen flatline again.

I exited my body and flew through the wall and kissed my mom, Jazmine, and said, "I'll be home soon, Mom. Hang in there..."

When I came back to the mountain, I had fallen. My leg was broken.

Bernette and Greg helped me rise to my feet. I was so happy I had only a broken leg, as I knew this fall could have killed me. So we made our way down to where my truck was parked. I reached into the back of my truck, grabbed my contractor megaphone and strapped it to my back. This megaphone had a curly wire connected to a Walkie-Talkie.

With the megaphone strapped to my back, I handed a paint brush to Bernette and said, "Write on all my windows."

She painted all kinds of words on my windshield and windows with all kinds of colors, all kinds of plants. The words she wrote were words like "Dream, Passion, Vision, Purpose, Freedom."

I knew I had to take my army home with me, but I wasn't sure how. I knew they were partially a figment of my imagination, and partially in a different timeline. In fact, I'm not really sure how this timeline plays into my near death experience. The Narrator talked about it like it was real. Almost as if in ten years I would be doing this same thing again just from a different perception. Much like how in The Fear Room I relived past memories over and over from a different perception.

I also knew from The Fear Room that I get shocked three times and on the third time I woke up to The Narrator. I assume on the third shock I will wake up to my real life as a teenage boy, so my time was short. Greg helped me sit on the roof on my truck. I stared at my army, now gathered to hear my words. I had to really encourage them.

I turned on the sound system in my truck and opened all the doors. I turned it all the way up and played instrumental music. I waved an imaginary conductor's wand and began conducting an orchestra in my mind.

I wanted this music in the background to clear my head before I began my speech.

The music began and I took a few seconds to savor this sacred moment. I believe in the power of art. I believe in the power of music. So often music is used to express thing we humans understand such as drugs, sex, alcohol. Music has the power to move you emotionally to a place of understanding you couldn't come to without it.

My army was all staring back at me all with turquoise eyes. They all believed. I took the Walkie-Talkie and began. I began this speech to humanity.

"Some say this is a dream, some say this is an alternate timeline, SOME say this is A REVOLUTION! BUT IT DOESN'T MATTER WHAT EACH OF US SAY AS INDIVIDUALS! It

only matters what we say collectively, together. As one unit. As one spirit! Because that's what humans do! We work together.

"If we don't have each other in this realm, then WHAT DO WE HAVE?! Live together, or die alone. We will stand on the solid rock, and destroy all the evil that has plagued this world. Humans have worked together since the beginning, and somewhere along the way we have lost our purpose.

"Our dreams have been snuffed out of us since we were kids. And since we were kids, we have been programmed to survive on the dreams of others, these dreams of other people that enslave us to lives of service. Slavery to the idea instead of the action.

I continued, "Our dreams have been snuffed out of us since we were kids, And since we were kids, we have been programmed to survive on the dreams of others. Dreams of other people enslave us to live a life of service to the idea instead of the action.Well, I say this is our dream! I say we decide where to go from here. Even if we're separated by different timelines, I will come back for you someway or another and until then, if you still exist when I leave Greg will lead you. I'm not sure what's going to happen. But I know you guys are capable of making change."

As Greg knelt down, I smiled at him. We will always share a connection. What a great man to be the way he is after his dad, Chris, raped him on his 7th birthday. Sometimes it's very hard not to focus on a person's pain instead of their healing and right now Greg is free and well. I just wish I could bring justice to his dad as I did Tusk.

I looked at the faces of so many people that were in chains not very long ago. Now that everyone had such purpose and such a desire to follow me into the future, I couldn't help but feel like I was about to abandon them. The good thing was that when I wake up as a boy, I'll have ten years to figure out a plan to save everyone. Beside that I don't have to worry too much, I know The Narrator will lead me down the right path. After all that's what this whole thing is about; getting me ready for my future. I get the feeling that things are just beginning for me.

"I say we work together again! As we worked together during the industrial revolution, we did it when we made the first airplane. WE DID IT WHEN WE WENT TO WAR OVER MONEY AND FUEL RIGHTS! NOW... STANDING BEFORE YOU, I ASK YOU... ON THIS DAY, TO STAND, STAND TOGETHER! NOT FOR MONEY! NOT FOR PRIDE! BUT FOR FREEDOM! FOR TRUTH! FOR CONNECTION TO EACH OTHER AND CONNECTION TO THE THINGS ABOVE. TO WALK WITH THE NARRATOR. TO WALK WITH EACH OTHER.

"Don't lose faith in this alternate timeline, I won't forget you are here when I go back home.

"That is where I'm headed, back home to my family. They need me and I need them. They deserve all of me, as does The Narrator. I'm not leaving you behind, but I'm leaving you to look forward to meeting what lies ahead on the path in front of you, and to have the faith to face your battles as I have demonstrated today, with you by my side. I thank you.

"I want you to know, you can make your timeline better! You have the spirit within you. There is no difference between you and me. I thank you from the bottom of my heart for being characters of my imagination. In helping me slay my enemies, that were tormenting me in my realm! Your spirits do exist in this other dimension. Your timeline does exist! I don't quite understand how all this works. I just know I'm not in it for much longer. It's been an honor being bound in chains together, but more than anything it's been an honor breaking our chains together. It's been an honor fighting evil together. Be at peace. I must return to my reality."

As I heard my army roar with the power of 100,000 men I smiled in respect for my new friends. Right as I finished this last look at my people in this timeline I was at peace. I heard the loud voice of the doctor speak one final time.

"1, 2, 3, CLEAR!"

BOOM

I was back. I noticed the screen start jumping around. I began to hear my heart beeping on the monitor. All the doctors were nervous at first, also they were on guard as they stood by

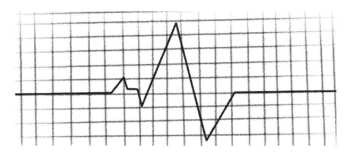

ready to shock me again. But once I had stabilized, they were relieved and tried to get me to talk.

I couldn't really find any words to say. I had been through so much already I was kinda stuck in my head for a while and I was okay with that. Me being alive and stabilized should be sufficient for the time being. I'm just relieved to be home again. I was exhausted. Right as I saw my mom, I drifted off to sleep.

Home Sweet Home:

Chapter 19

Iopened my eyes to reality. I guess I was sleeping overnight. I awoke to a new perception of my reality. My mom was sleeping on my stomach and my dad, Abraham, was sleeping on the couch.

I immediately looked in the mirror over the sink that was on the wall next to my bed and looked at my face. It's me. The real me, I think. I mean, my hair is brown again as a kid. I had white dreads in my dreams. I definitely feel a bit unstable, or maybe that's just my "perception." Maybe this is the new me. The little bit crazy side of me. Maybe this isn't crazy, maybe you could call it "enlightened."

See, enlightenment is as strange as it may seem. Sometimes I feel like The Narrator is still a part of me, and the spirit dancer is also still dancing around, leading me.

"Mom, Dad," I said softly.

Their heads shot up so fast, I wouldn't have thought they were asleep.

"Son!" my dad exclaimed, "I'm so sorry. We almost lost you."

"Dad, it's okay."

"It's okay? No, it's not! You tried to kill yourself!"

Jazmine quickly intervened, "Abraham, Hon, let our son gather himself. He's been through a lot. Baby, we're just glad you're alive, that's all that matters right now."

"I'm glad to be alive and be here with you Mom, and you Dad."

"Kev," my dad began, "I'm sorry I told you about the divorce alone. I'm sorry I was drunk. That's not the way I wanted to handle it. It was all just too much for me. Through all these hard times, when we didn't know what was going to happen to you, me and your mom could see how this was too hard on you.

"Kevin, your mom and I love you and our family's happiness is all that matters. We have decided to work things out."

"I am so relieved," I thought to myself.

I must tell them about what I just experienced.

"MOM! DAD! I need to tell you! I must tell you I had a near death experience. I lived a whole life and killed evil spirits and had an army! I had this amazing armor. I had a wife and kids. I lived an entire life and it's this life I'm going to end up living out right in front of my Twerky eyes."

"'Twerky eyes?' What does that mean?"

"Uh, I thought 'twerky' is the new brown, Bahaha!" I said as I rolled my eyes and turned my face. Looking into the mirror my faith said my eyes were turquoise still.

"Woah, woah, twerky? Killing evil and killing armies and making babies, kid, that's a bit much right now. Let's discuss this at home.

"Son, I love you, but you have been through a lot. I think you need more rest. Is there anything I can get you?"

"All I want is to go home and see my sisters," I explained.

Jazmine said, "Let me talk to the doctors. You have been asleep for almost 24 hours. I'll see if we can go home."

As Mom and Dad went to talk to the doctors, I began thinking of all I just went through. All the pain, the fear, and trauma but also all the victory. I know that all those souls I saved will not go through the trauma in ten years. I killed all The Door Masters, but I know there are other Door Masters in hidden galaxies and realms. I must find a way to get my story out. Hmmm, I'll think on it.

My mom came back in with a tissue to her eyes and said, "Kev, Dad's going to get your sisters from aunt Amber's house. The doctors are going to monitor you for a few more hours and then we can leave."

"Okay, Mom. I understand."

I thought to myself, "What's a few more hours when I just spent a lifetime in another world?"

When the time came they insisted on wheeling me out of the hospital even though I felt perfectly fine. Then me and my mom drove away.On the way home, we stopped to get some food at my favorite restaurant. I couldn't help but be excited to be home.

"Mom... I love you so much. I missed you."

Mom replied, "I love you too, Kevin."

My dad had my sisters in his truck and was meeting us at the restaurant. When we all shuffled into our table I kissed Carrie and Seymer. I don't think they knew too much as they didn't say much, but they were happy to see me.

I started to think hard about The Narrator and The Mime. I missed them so much. This is the hardest part, I loved my family but I also loved everyone from my dream. My army, the lost souls. We grew close as we all were freed together. We all stood by each other and destroyed all the evil in that realm... wherever it was. I didn't want to fail them, I knew in ten years something bad was going to happen to everyone in the trauma room... If not all the rooms. I couldn't think of anything I could do at 14 years old, when none of this was to take place till I was 24.

"Hmmm," I thought to myself.

Exhausted from absolutely nothing coming to mind I snapped out of it when I noticed our food had arrived. Carrie and Seymer started clapping. They had both been sitting next to me holding my hands. I can only imagine the trauma they went through hearing about their brother and how he may die. I felt so stupid. I looked at my bandaged arm and remembered what I had done.

"Mom… Dad… I'm sorry for what I put you through."

My dad said, "Son, we forgive you. But are you okay? Like really okay?"

I replied, "I feel okay, I don't know what came over me."

My dad began to tell me saying, "Son, the hospital is requiring that you see a psychiatrist, be evaluated, and go to a support group. There's a session every week and it just so happens to fall onto tonight. I want you to go. Who knows, you may like it."

I replied, "Hmm… I'll have to think about it…"

He interrupted, "Son, this one's not up for discussion… you're going. I want you to talk about your near-death experience."

I thought to myself, "Near death experience? Is that what I had? I'm going to look into this further immediately after I get home.

Man, I wish I knew everyone could understand the amount of therapy I just got going through this experience. At the same time, I understand how scared my parents must feel when I think about my kids, 'Rayne and Matthew.' The ones

I'm going to have in ten years. Just thinking about them sent a calming sensation through my body and I replied 'I understand, Dad. I'll go.'"

He replied "Well…. Good. We will enjoy our food and head home to rest up. We will head to your support group at 7:00 pm. Sounds good, kid?"

I took a bite and said, "Sounds good" with food in my mouth.

We headed home after our waitress brought our check to the table. It wasn't a long ride home. The hospital was in a suburb of Denver. I felt the bumpy road that led to our house.I was so excited when we headed up our driveway and I saw our beautiful home. I slammed the door and ran upstairs, immediately I opened my laptop to google "near-death experiences." What came up was amazing. I clicked on link after link. I read stories about it and read a lot about DMT.

Everything made sense now. I officially had a DMT experience.

I researched until I fell asleep.

"Kevin! Are you ready for the support group!? We're running late, let's go!" My dad said as he smacked on my door.

"Coming… Dad." I said, waking from a deep sleep.

Recovery:

Chapter 20

I put my journal in my backpack and got dressed quickly, as I heard my dad shout again, "Kevin! Come on, we're going to be late!"

"I'm coming, Dad!" I yelled as I ran down the stairs.

When we go in the car everything calmed down as this church was only 10 minutes away. My dad is a very "early is on time" type of a guy, and we had 10 minutes to spare.

"Great," I thought to myself, "I'm the new guy coming in early."

At this point, nothing really bothers me like it used to. I'm much more patient as I'm so happy to be home and alive.

When we pulled up to the church my dad said "Okay, Kevin. Don't be shy and really lean into this. You are not the only one there that has done something like this. This is a support group for suicidal and depressed teens. The support group leader is named Chuck. He said they meet in the cafeteria which is the second door on the right. Do you want me to walk you in?"

"No thanks. I got it, Dad. I'll see you at 9:00."

"Alright, kid, see ya then. Call me if you need anything."

I shut the door and began to feel a bit nervous. I walked briskly to the front door and stepped in confidently as I have been through much more terrifying doors than the doors of a church, however scary a church may be.

I walked through and everything was as it should be. No crazy Door Master or trapped prisoners. There was a picture of a white-bearded man with long hair that looked like a mixture of a handsome model and the Mona Lisa. I guess this was supposed to be the man they call Jesus.

There was a bible on the table below the picture and I walked by all of it as I had no interest in the religious figure. I had a connection to the real deal, The Narrator. I walked straight to the second door on my right just like my dad said. I saw a full-grown man setting up chairs in a big circle.

I kinda gave a little knock and said, "Hi, are you 'Chuck'?"

He turned around and gave a chuckle and said "Chuck? No, you mean Chris? You must be Kevin! Nice to meet you! I'm the youth minister at Bread of Life Pentecostal Church.

"Welcome to God's country! Hallelujah! Hallelujah! Welcome! Come in, sit! Sit! Your dad was in touch with me and told me a little about what happened. Since we have some time to spare, maybe we could get to know each other."

His face was oddly familiar and gave me bad vibes, but I couldn't quite put my finger on it.

So I hesitated, then said, "Sure."

He responded well. "How are you, Kevin?"

I said, "I'm good… I'm thankful to be home with my family. I really screwed up last night. I'm so happy for My mom and dad there staying together, and my baby sisters. I love my sisters so much. It would have crushed them to find out about my parents' divorce. They are such precious girls."

He responded in a nice voice, "Yes, kids are great. Me and my wife had a miscarriage a year ago and are trying to have another baby now. Ya know how that goes… Haha… Anyway, we hope to get pregnant in the next couple years. We already have names picked out. If we have a girl we're thinking of the name 'Gabrielle.' If we have a boy, we're going to name him 'Greg.'"

My face dropped, I thought to myself "I knew there was something off about this guy! THIS IS THE MAN THAT RAPES GREG IN TEN YEARS!!!

This is no coincidence. My mission has begun. But first I gotta get away from here. So I quickly interrupted and asked where the restroom was.

Chris said, "It was the first door to your right when you came in."

I replied, "Okay, I'll be right back. I passed the bathroom and went straight outside and sat next to a tree on the side of the church and started writing down every lesson and person I encountered in my near-death experience. I had no intention of going back inside, but I knew I had too when I remembered that Chris hasn't necessarily done anything wrong yet when his son hasn't even been born.

After I wrote down everything I could remember, I went inside very late. When I walked in, I stood in the back quietly, but Chris saw me and said "Hey, Kevin! I'm glad you decided to join us feel free to stay where you are and observe for tonight if you're uncomfortable."

I replied, "Sure, thanks."

Chris continued his meeting with about 10 other kids my age, maybe a little younger.

They went around the room talking about their struggles confiding in Chris and telling him about their pain. I noticed some kids were uncomfortable and wouldn't look him in the eyes or talk. He didn't push them either.

I was suspicious of all this: of Chris, of the safety of the kids. I thought me walking through this door was different, but it wasn't. I finally realized this was a very scary door with a very scary Door Master named Chris, and Chris was in authority of 10 very, very naive prisoners. My mission has begun and I must do something. When he dismissed the class, I went straight outside to meet my dad.

Dad picked me up and asked me how things went, like dads should. I gave him the typical answers a teenager would. When I got home my mom was already sleeping and so were my sisters, everyone was very tired from everything. My dad got a snack from the kitchen as I sat on the living room couch thinking and processing everything that happened in the support group.

I am just so exhausted from everything that I've been through lately, I figured it would be best if I let my mind rest. I have been on an emotional rollercoaster for so long I cannot process things accurately.

I made up my mind. I'm going to bed. So I went into my restroom to wash my face and brush my teeth. As I was cleaning my hands off I couldn't help but notice this tall decor stand with magazines on it, this was next to the toilet and sink, of course. This had always been there, but something stood out this time.

There it was! It was the turquoise color that caught my attention. I couldn't help but think of those beautiful eyes, The Narrator's eyes. Eyes of artistic design and purpose. Then I thought about my whole experience again and how I lead an army that would be facing trauma in ten years. I also thought about the prisoners in the church of Chris The Door Master.

I said to myself, "I have to do something to help them, maybe there's a sign in this magazine? After all, it is turquoise... just a coincidence? Let's find out!"

I picked up this magnificent colored magazine next to me and thought to myself, "See, I have a purpose in life. A place in the overall painting, this is from my "perception" or "desire" to better understand myself as a human being. This is what we are all simultaneously trying to accomplish, right?

"I see myself as a painter of a masterpiece canvas, and this canvas is me, and the strokes of life are the color of my experience. It's the bigger picture, the broad spectrum of things is how my mind works now.

"That's it!" I thought.

"I'm looking for a sign in this magazine like some kind of text or book that will give me some answers. But the answer wasn't written anywhere... That is the answer! I can write my story! My story! My book! My great battles! This is a legendary story that will heal many, just as it healed me. This will be a masterpiece!"

I went back into my bedroom and pulled my journal out of my backpack and got to work.

"Okay, what's a good name for this story," I thought to myself, "Okay. Think, Kevin. We had fear, a Door Master in my face, Tusk in my face, The Narrator in my face... and it was a terribly wonderful long DMT experience, a near-death experience also like a dream...."

That's when I heard a voice tell me a specific name, and it clicked. That's it! I looked at the white piece of paper and began to write the title and preface of my new book. This is what the voice told me to call my story. That's it! It's perfect! I had to write it down!

When I finished writing the preface of my soon to be book, I looked over and my bedroom mirror beside my desk. I kept my eyes closed for 7 seconds and could see The Mime dancing in the cosmos. When I opened them, I believed everything was real and for a split second my eyes glitched a bright turquoise color and I smiled… I began to read the intro…

Finishing Touch:

Chapter 21

"Masterpiece: Volume 1,
   Fear in The Face of a Dying Dream."

Preface

Third Level of Understanding:

As I stare into my canvas, I see how each brush stroke makes such a difference.

Every time I change my mind on the direction, I realize that every stroke has a specific purpose, a place in the overall painting. For the greater good, I should say. What if I randomly splatter a pointless stroke of disaster? Another way I could look at this question is, could this be nothing more than a stroke of luck? Ohh that's good. Wait, that couldn't work unless I make it work of course. Interesting concept, I like this concept rather well actually.

See, we all have these expectations in life, these "labeled boxes" that we put our personal experiences in. What a beautiful picture of how we all play a personal role, a personal part in this story we call life. The proof is, we do all have different expectations don't we? Great! We agree on this matter then. This reminds me of my whole point. Humanity, please bear with me, as I know we're all tired of the cliché philosophical RA-RA that were unbelievably used to in life. However, humanity is all we as a race seem to understand on a surface level. Perhaps, our perception of humanity is only a figment of your imagination. I feel the word "imagination" comes across too colorful in this context. I think "desire" may better express what I mean. A "desire" to better understand ourselves as humans is what we all simultaneously are trying to accomplish.

This brings me to my secondary point. See, I think... no, I "desire" that there is more to the human race than what meets the naked eye. Lastly, My tri-angular point in the opening of this book, or maybe it's more of an offer to you as the individual reader. Follow me into my dream, my masterpiece painting of a canvas. Literally, with your heart's permission, I will take you on a journey to the center of the canvas. This canvas is you. This canvas is me. Your life is the strokes of the brush that provide the color of your life. Your life that we think of as our "personal" experiences. Be warned! Don't get lost or lose your way as this is an artistic journey. Try and keep up to not only to what the tri-eye can see, but what is beyond deep, deep into the subconscious of what you "perceive" as the human race. Still, as humanity remains a singular consciousness, yet separated by personal but very unique energetic entities. This is exactly as strange as you "perceive" this to be. Still, I ask to follow me into the colorful life of a boy named

Kevin,
The End

Made in the USA
Middletown, DE
23 December 2019

81820132R00111